D1056558

# THEODORE STURGEON

# THE

# DREAMING

# JEWELS

Theodore Sturgeon was born on February 26, 1918, in Staten Island, New York, and died in Eugene, Oregon, May 8, 1985. He lived in New York City, upstate New York, and Los Angeles. He is the author of *More Than Human*, winner of the International Fantasy Award; *Venus Plus X*; *To Marry Medusa*, which was also published under the title *The Cosmic Rape*; *The Dreaming Jewels*; and numerous other books and stories. He won the Hugo and Nebula Awards for his short story "Slow Sculpture" and the World Fantasy Life Achievement Award.

## Also by THEODORE STURGEON

*More Than Human*
*I, Libertine*
*Venus Plus X*
*To Marry Medusa*
*Some of Your Blood*
*Godbody*

*The Complete Stories of Theodore Sturgeon:*
Volume I: *The Ultimate Egoist*
Volume II: *Microcosmic God*
Volume III: *Killdozer!*
Volume IV: *Thunder and Roses*
Volume V: *The Perfect Host*

# THE
# DREAMING
# JEWELS

## THEODORE STURGEON

VINTAGE BOOKS

A DIVISION OF RANDOM HOUSE, INC.

NEW YORK

FIRST VINTAGE BOOKS EDITION, OCTOBER 1999

*Copyright © 1950 by Theodore Sturgeon*
*Copyright renewed 1978 by the Theodore Sturgeon Literary Trust*

All rights reserved under International and Pan-American copyright
conventions. Published in the United States by Vintage Books,
a division of Random House, Inc., New York, and simultaneously
in Canada by Random House of Canada Limited, Toronto.
Originally published in hardcover in the United States by
Greenberg, Publisher, New York, in 1950.

Vintage and colophon are registered trademarks of
Random House, Inc.

Library of Congress Cataloging-in-Publication Data
Sturgeon, Theodore.
The dreaming jewels / Theodore Sturgeon. — 1st Vintage Books ed.
p. cm.
ISBN 0-375-70373-X
I. Title.
PS3569.T875D7 1999
813'.54—dc21 99-25700
CIP

www.vintagebooks.com

Printed in the United States of America
10 9 8 7 6 5 4 3 2

# THE
# DREAMING
# JEWELS

THEY CAUGHT THE KID DOING SOMETHING disgusting out under the bleachers at the high-school stadium, and he was sent home from the grammar school across the street. He was eight years old then. He'd been doing it for years.

In a way it was a pity. He was a nice kid, a nice-looking kid too, though not particularly outstanding. There were other kids, and teachers, who liked him a little bit, and some who disliked him a little bit; but everyone jumped on him when it got around. His name was Horty—Horton, that is—Bluett. Naturally he caught blazes when he got home.

He opened the door as quietly as he could, but they heard him, and hauled him front and center into the living room where he stood flushing, with his head down, one sock around his ankle, and his arms full of books and a catcher's mitt. He was a good catcher, for an eight-year-old. He said, "I was—"

"We know," said Armand Bluett. Armand was a bony individual with a small mustache and cold wet eyes. He clapped his hands to his forehead and then threw up his arms. "My God, boy, what in Heaven's name made you do a filthy thing like that?" Armand Bluett was not a religious man, but he always talked like that when he clapped his hands to his head, which he did quite often.

Horty did not answer. Mrs. Bluett, whose name was Tonta, sighed and asked for a highball. She did not smoke, and needed a substitute for the smoker's thoughtful match-lit pause when she was at a loss for words. She was so seldom at a loss for words that a fifth of rye lasted her six weeks. She and Armand were not Horton's parents. Horton's parents were upstairs, but the Bluetts did not know it. Horton was allowed to call Armand and Tonta by their first names.

"Might I ask," said Armand icily, "how long you have had this nauseating habit? Or was it an experiment?"

Horty knew they weren't going to make it easy on him. There was the same puckered expression on

Armand's face as when he tasted wine and found it unexpectedly good.

"I don't do it much," Horty said, and waited.

"May the Lord have mercy on us for our generosity in taking in this little swine," said Armand, clapping his hands to his head again. Horty let his breath out. Now that was over with. Armand said it every time he was angry. He marched out to mix Tonta a highball.

"Why did you do it, Horty?" Tonta's voice was more gentle only because her vocal cords were more gently shaped than her husband's. Her face showed the same implacable cold.

"Well, I—just felt like it, I guess." Horty put his books and catcher's mitt down on the footstool.

Tonta turned her face away from him and made an unspellable, retching syllable. Armand strode back in, bearing a tinkling glass.

"Never heard anything like it in my life," he said scornfully. "I suppose it's all over the school?"

"I guess so."

"The children? The teachers too, no doubt. But of course. Anyone say anything to you?"

"Just Dr. Pell." He was the principal. "He said—said they could . . ."

"Speak up!"

Horty had been through it once. Why, why go through it all again? "He said the school could get along without f-filthy savages."

"I can understand how he felt," Tonta put in, smugly.

"And what about the other kids? They say anything?"

"Hecky brought me some worms. And Jimmy called me Sticky-tongue." And Kay Hallowell had laughed, but he didn't mention that.

"Sticky-tongue. Not bad, that, for a kid. Ant-eater." Again the hand clapped against the brow. "My God, what am I going to do if Mr. Anderson greets me with 'Hi Sticky-tongue!' Monday morning? This will be all over town, sure as God made little apples." He fixed Horty with the sharp wet points of his gaze. "And do you plan to take up bug-eating as a profession?"

"They weren't bugs," Horty said diffidently and with accuracy. "They were ants. The little brown kind."

Tonta choked on her highball. "Spare us the details."

"My God," Armand said again, "what'll he grow up as?" He mentioned two possibilities. Horty understood one of them. The other made even the knowledgeable Tonta jump. "Get out of here."

Horty went to the stairs while Armand thumped down exasperatedly beside Tonta. "I've had mine," he said. "I'm full up to here. That brat's been the symbol of failure to me ever since I laid eyes on his dirty face. This place isn't big enough—*Horton!*"

"Huh."

"Come back here and take your garbage with you. I don't want to be reminded that you're in the house."

Horty came back slowly, staying out of Armand Bluett's reach, picked up his books and the catcher's mitt, dropped a pencil-box—at which Armand my-

Godded again—picked it up, almost dropped the mitt, and finally fled up the stairs.

"The sins of the stepfathers," said Armand, "are visited on the stepfathers, even unto the thirty-fourth irritation. What have I done to deserve this?"

Tonta swirled her drink, keeping her eyes on it and her lips pursed appreciatively as she did so. There had been a time when she disagreed with Armand. Later, there was a time when she disagreed and said nothing. All that had been too wearing. Now she kept an appreciative exterior and let it soak in as deeply as it would. Life was so much less trouble that way.

Once in his room, Horty sank down on the edge of the bed with his arms still full of his books. He did not close the door because there was none, due to Armand's conviction that privacy was harmful for youngsters. He did not turn on the light because he knew everything in the room, knew it with his eyes closed. There was little enough. Bed, dresser, closet with a cracked cheval glass. A child's desk, practically a toy, that he had long outgrown. In the closet were three oiled-silk dress-covers stuffed full of Tonta's unused clothes, which left almost no space for his.

His . . .

None of this was really his. If there had been a smaller room, he would have been shoved into it. There were two guest bedrooms on this floor, and another above, and they almost never had guests. The clothes he wore weren't his; they were concessions to something Armand called "my position in this town"; rags would have done if it weren't for that.

He rose, the act making him conscious of the clutter he still clutched in his arms. He put it down on the bed. The mitt was his, though. He'd bought it for seventy-five cents from the Salvation Army store. He got the money by hanging around Dempledorff's market and carrying packages for people, a dime a trip. He had thought Armand would be pleased; he was always talking about resourcefulness and earning ability. But he had forbidden Horty ever to do that again. "My God! People will think we are paupers!" So the mitt was all he had to show for the episode.

All he had in the world—except, of course, Junky.

He looked, through the half-open closet door, at the top shelf and its clutter of Christmas-tree lights (the Christmas tree was outside the house, where the neighbors could see—never inside), old ribbons, a lampshade, and—Junky.

He pulled the oversized chair away from the undersized desk and carried it—if he had dragged it, Armand would have been up the stairs two at a time to see what he was up to, and if it was fun, would have forbidden it—and set it down carefully in the closet doorway. Standing on it, he felt behind the leftovers on the shelf until he found the hard square bulk of Junky. He drew it out, a cube of wood, gaudily painted and badly chipped, and carried it to the desk.

Junky was the kind of toy so well-known, so well-worn, that it was not necessary to see it frequently, or touch it often, to know that it was there. Horty was a foundling—found in a park one late fall evening, with only a receiving blanket tucked about him. He had acquired Junky while he was at the Home, and when he had been chosen by Armand as an adoptee (during Armand's campaign for City Counsellor, which he lost, but which he thought would be helped along if it were known he had adopted a "poor little homeless waif") Junky was part of the bargain.

Horty put Junky softly on the desk and touched a worn stud at the side. Violently at first, then with rusted-spring hesitancy, and at last defiantly, Junky emerged, a jack-in-the-box, a refugee from a more gentle generation. He was a Punch, with a chipped hooked nose which all but met his upturned, pointed chin. In the gulch between these stretched a knowing smile.

But all Junky's personality—and all his value to Horty—was in his eyes. They seemed to have been cut, or molded, blunt-faceted, from some leaded glass which gave them a strange, complex glitter, even in the dimmest room. Time and again Horty had been certain that those eyes had a radiance of their own, though he could never quite be sure.

He murmured, "Hi, Junky."

The jack-in-the-box nodded with dignity, and Horty reached and caught its smooth chin. "Junky, let's get away from here. Nobody wants us. Maybe we wouldn't get anything to eat, and maybe we'd be cold, but gee . . . Think of it, Junky. Not being scared when we hear *his* key in the lock, and never sitting at dinner while he asks questions until we have to lie, and—and all like that." He did not have to explain himself to Junky.

He let the chin go, and the grinning head bobbed up and down, and then nodded slowly, thoughtfully.

"They shouldn't 'a been like that about the ants," Horty confided. "I didn't *drag* nobuddy to see. Went off by myself. But that stinky Hecky, he's been watching me. An' then he sneaked off and got Mr. Carter. That was no way to do, now was it, Junky?" He tapped the head on the side of its hooked nose, and it shook its head agreeably. "I hate a sneak."

"You mean me, no doubt," said Armand Bluett from the doorway.

Horty didn't move, and for a long instant his heart didn't either. He half crouched, half cowered behind the desk, not turning toward the doorway.

"What are you doing?"

"Nothin'."

Armand belted him across the cheek and ear. Horty whimpered, once, and bit his lip. Armand said, "Don't lie. You are obviously doing something. You were talking to yourself, a sure sign of a degenerating mind. What's this—oh. Oh yes, the baby toy that came with you. Your estate. It's as repulsive as you are." He took it from the desk, dropped it on the floor, wiped his hand on the side of his trousers, and carefully stepped on Junky's head.

Horty shrieked as if it were his own head which was being crushed, and leapt at Armand. So unexpected was the attack that the man was bowled right off his feet. He fell heavily and painfully against the bedpost, grabbed at it and missed, and went to the floor. He sat there for a moment grunting and blinking, and then his little eyes narrowed and fixed themselves on the trembling Horty. "Mmm—*hm!*" said Armand in a tone of great satisfaction, and rose. "You should be exterminated." He grasped the slack of Horty's shirt and struck him. As he spoke, he hit the boy's face, back and forth, back and forth, by way of punctuation. "Homicidal, that's what you are. I was going to. Send you away. To a school. But it isn't safe. The police will. Take care of you. They have a place. For juvenile delinquents. Filthy little. Pervert."

He rushed the sodden child across the room and jammed him into the closet. "This will keep you safe until the police get here," he panted, and slammed the door. The hinge side of it caught three fingers of Horty's left hand.

At the boy's shriek of very real agony Armand snapped the door open again. "No use in your yelling. You—My God! What a mess. Now I suppose I'll have to get a doctor. There's no end—absolutely **no** end to the trouble you cause. Tonta!" He ran out and down the stairs. "Tonta!"

"Yes, Peaches."

"That young devil stuck his hand in the door. Did it on purpose, to excite sympathy. Bleeding like a stuck pig. You know what he did? He struck me. He attacked me, Tonta! It's not safe to have him in the house!"

"You poor darling! Did he hurt you?"

"A wonder he didn't kill me. I'm going to call the police."

"I'd better go up while you're phoning," said Tonta. She wet her lips.

But when she reached the room, Horty was gone. There was a lot of excitement for a while after that. At first Armand wanted to get his hands on Horty for his own purposes, and then he began to be afraid of what people might say if the boy gave his own garbled version of the incident. Then a day went by, and a week, and a month, and it was safe to look to heaven and say mysteriously, "He's in safe hands now, the poor little tyke," and people could answer, "I understand . . ." Everyone knew he was not Armand's child, anyway.

But Armand Bluett tucked one idea snugly away in the corner of his mind. That was to look out, in the future, for any young man with three fingers missing from his left hand.

THE HALLOWELLS LIVED AT THE EDGE
of town, in a house that had only one thing wrong
with it; it was at the intersection where the State
Highway angled into the end of Main Street, so that
the traffic roared night and day past both the front
and back gates.

The Hallowell's taffy-headed daughter, Kay, was
as full of social consciousness as only a seven-year-
old can be. She had been asked to empty the trash,

and as usual she opened the back gate a crack and peeped out at the highway, to see if anyone she knew would catch her at the menial task.

"*Horty!*"

He shrank into the fog-swirled shadows of the traffic-light standard.

"Horton Bluett, I see you."

"Kay . . ." He came to her, staying close to the fence. "Listen, don't tell nobody you saw me, huh?"

"But wh—oh. You're running away!" she blurted, noticing the parcel tucked under his arm. "Horty— are you sick?" He was white, strained. "Did you hurt your hand?"

"Some." He held his left wrist with his right hand, tightly. His left hand was wrapped in two or three handkerchiefs. "They was going to get the police. I got out the window onto the shed roof and hid there all afternoon. They was lookin' all over the street and everywhere. You won't tell?"

"I won't tell. What's in the package?"

"Nothin'."

If she had demanded it, grabbed at it, he would probably never have seen her again. Instead she said, "Please, Horty."

"You can look." Without releasing his wrist, he turned so she could pull the package out from under his arm. She opened it—it was a paper bag—and took out the hideous broken face of Junky. Junky's eyes glittered at her, and she squeaked. "What is it?"

"It's Junky. I had him since before I was born. Armand, he stepped on it."

"Is that why you're running away?"

"*Kay! What are you doing out there?*"

"Coming, Mother! Horty, I got to go. Horty, are you coming back?"

"Not *ever.*"

"Gee . . . that mister Bluett, he's so *mean* . . ."

*Kay Hallowell! Come in this instant. It's raining!*"

"Yes, Mother! Horty, I wannit to tell you. I shouldn'ta laughed at you today. Hecky brought you the worms, and I thought it was a joke, thass all. I didn't know you really did eat ants. Gee . . . I et some shoe-polish once. That's nothin'."

Horty held out his elbow and she carefully put the package under it. He said, as if he had just thought of it—and indeed he had—"I *will* come back, Kay. Someday."

"*Kay!*"

" 'Bye, Horty." And she was gone, a flash of taffy hair, yellow dress, a bit of lace, changed before his eyes to a closed gate in a board fence and the sound of dwindling quick footsteps.

Horton Bluett stood in the dark drizzle, cold, but with heat in his ruined hand and another heat in his throat. This he swallowed, with difficulty, and, looking up, saw the broad inviting tailgate of a truck which was stopped for the traffic light. He ran to it, tossed his small bundle on it, and squirmed up, clawing with his right hand, trying to keep his left out of trouble. The truck lurched forward; Horty scrabbled wildly to stay on. The package with Junky in it began to slide back toward him, past him; he caught at it, losing his own grip, and began to slip.

Suddenly there was a blur of movement from inside the truck, and a flare of terrible pain as his smashed hand was caught in a powerful grip. He came very close to fainting; when he could see again he was lying on his back on the jolting floor of the truck, holding his wrist again, expressing his anguish in squeezed-out tears and little, difficult grunts.

"Gee, kid, you don't care how long you live, do you?" It was a fat boy, apparently his own age, bending over him, his bowed head resting on three chins. "What's the matter with your hand?"

Horty said nothing. He was quite beyond speech for the moment. The fat boy, with surprising gentleness, pressed Horty's good hand away from the handkerchiefs and began laying back the cloth. When he got to the inner layer, he saw the blood by the wash of light from a street-light they passed, and he said "Man."

When they stopped for another traffic signal at a lighted intersection, he looked carefully and said, "Oh, man," with all the emphasis inside him somewhere, and his eyes contracted into two pitying little knots of wrinkles. Horty knew the fat boy was sorry for him, and only then did he begin to cry openly. He wished he could stop, but he couldn't, and didn't while the boy bound up his hand again and for quite a while afterward.

The fat boy sat back on a roll of new canvas to wait for Horty to calm down. Once Horty subsided a little and the boy winked at him, and Horty, profoundly susceptible to the least kindness, began to wail again. The boy picked up the paper bag, looked into it, grunted, closed it carefully and put it out of

the way on the canvas. Then to Horty's astonishment, he removed from his inside coat pocket a large
silver cigar case, the kind with five metal cylinders
built together, took out a cigar, put it all in his mouth
and turned it to wet it down, and lit up, surrounding
himself with sweet-acrid blue smoke. He did not try
to talk, and after a while Horty must have dozed off,
because he opened his eyes to find the fat boy's
jacket folded as a pillow under his head, and he
could not remember its being put there. It was dark
then; he sat up, and immediately the fat boy's voice
came from the blackness.

"Take it easy, kid." A small pudgy hand steadied
Horty's back. "How do you feel?"

Horty tried to talk, choked, swallowed and tried
again. "All right, I guess. Hungry . . . gee! We're
out in the country!"

He became conscious of the fat boy squatting beside him. The hand left his back; in a moment the
flame of a match startled him, and for an etched moment the boy's face floated before him in the waver-
ing light, moonlike, with delicate pink lips acrawl on
the black cigar. Then with a practiced flick of his fingers, he sent the match and its brilliance flying out
into the night. "Smoke?"

"I never did smoke," said Horty. "Some corn-silk,
once." He looked admiringly at the red jewel at the
end of the cigar. "You smoke a lot, huh."

"Stunts m'growth," said the other, and burst into
a peal of shrill laughter. "How's the hand?"

"It hurts some. Not so bad."

"You got a lot of grit, kid. I'd be screamin' for morphine if I was you. What happened to it?"

Horty told him. The story came out in snatches, out of sequence, but the fat boy got it all. He questioned briefly, and to the point, and did not comment at all. The conversation died after he had asked as many questions as he apparently wanted to, and for a while Horty thought the other had dozed off. The cigar dimmed and dimmed, occasionally sputtering around the edges, once in a while brightening in a wavery fashion as vagrant air touched it from the back of the truck.

Abruptly, and in a perfectly wide-awake voice, the fat boy asked him, "You lookin' fer work?"

"Work? Well—I guess maybe."

"What made you eat them ants?" came next.

"Well, I—I don't know. I guess I just—well, I wanted to."

"Do you do that a lot?"

"Not too much." This was a different kind of questioning than he had had from Armand. The boy asked him about it without revulsion, without any more curiosity, really, than he had asked him how old he was, what grade he was in.

"Can you sing?"

"Well—I guess so. Some."

"Sing something. I mean, if you feel like it. Don't strain y'self. Uh—know *Stardust*?"

Horty looked out at the starlit highway racing away beneath the rumbling wheels, the blaze of yellow-white which turned to dwindling red tail-light eyes as a car whisked by on the other side of the road. The fog was gone, and a lot of the pain was gone from his hand, and most of all he was gone from Armand and Tonta. Kay had given him a feather-touch of kindness, and this odd boy, who talked in a way he had never heard a boy talk before, had given him another sort of kindness. There were the beginnings of a wonderful warm glow inside him, a feeling he had had only once or twice before in his whole life—the time he had won the sack-race and they gave him a khaki handkerchief, and the time four kids had whistled to a mongrel dog, and the dog had come straight to him, ignoring the others. He began to sing, and because the truck rumbled so, he had to sing out to be heard; and because he had to sing out, he leaned on the song, giving something of himself to it as a high-steel worker gives part of his weight to the wind.

He finished. The fat boy said "Hey." The unaccented syllable was warm praise. Without any further comment he went to the front of the truck body and thumped on the square pane of glass there. The truck immediately slowed, pulled over and stopped by the roadside. The fat boy went to the tailgate, sat down, and slid off to the road.

"You stay right there," he told Horty. "I'm gonna ride up front a while. You hear me now—don't go 'way."

"I won't," said Horty.

"How the hell can you sing like that with your hand mashed?"

"I don't know. It doesn't hurt so much now."

"Do you eat grasshoppers too? Worms?"

"No!" cried Horty, horrified.

"Okay," said the boy. He went to the cab of the truck; the door slammed, and the truck ground off again.

Horty worked his way carefully forward until, squatting by the front wall of the truck-body, he could see through the square pane.

The driver was a tall man with a curious skin, lumpy and grey-green. He had a nose like Junky's, but almost no chin, so that he looked like an aged parrot. He was so tall that he had to curve over the wheel like a fern-frond.

Next to him were two little girls. One had a round bush of white hair—no; it was platinum—and the other had two thick ropes of pigtails, bangs, and beautiful teeth. The fat boy was next to her, talking animatedly. The driver seemed not to pay any attention to the conversation at all.

Horty's head was not clear, but he did not feel sick either. Everything had an exciting, dreamlike quality. He moved back in the truck body and lay down with his head on the fat boy's jacket. Immediately he sat up, and crawled among the goods stacked in the truck until his hand found the long roll of canvas, moved along it until he found his paper bag. Then he lay down again, his left hand resting easily on his stomach, his right inside the bag, with his index and little fingers resting between Junky's nose and chin. He went to sleep.

WHEN HE WOKE AGAIN THE TRUCK HAD
stopped, and he opened unfocussed eyes to a writhing glare of light—red and orange, green and blue,
with an underlying sheet of dazzling gold.

He raised his head, blinking, and resolved the
lights into a massive post bearing neon signs: ICE
TWENTY FLAVORS CREAM and CABINS and
BAR—EAT. The wash of gold came from floodlights
over the service area of a gas station. Three tractor-

trailer trucks were drawn up behind the fat boy's truck; one of them had its trailer built of heavily-ribbed stainless steel and was very lovely under the lights.

"You awake, kid?"

"Uh—Hi! Yes."

"We're going to grab a bite. Come on."

Horty rose stiffly to his knees. He said, "I haven't got any money."

"Hell with that," said the fat boy. "Come on."

He put a firm hand under Horty's armpit as he climbed down. A jukebox throbbed behind the grinding sound of a gasoline pump, and their feet crunched pleasantly on cinders. "What's your name?" Horty asked.

"They call me Havana," said the fat boy. "I never been there. It's the cigars."

"My name's Horty Bluett."

"We'll change that."

The driver and the two girls were waiting for them by the door of a diner. Horty hardly had a chance to look at them before they all crowded through and lined up at the counter. Horty sat between the driver and the silver-haired girl. The other one, the one with dark ropes of braided hair took the next stool, and Havana, the fat-boy, sat at the end.

Horty looked first at the driver—looked, stared, and dragged his eyes away in the same tense moment. The driver's sagging skin was indeed a grey-green, dry, loose, leather-rough. He had pouches under his eyes, which were red and inflamed-looking, and his underlip drooped to show long white lower incisors.

The backs of his hands showed the same loose sage-green skin, though his fingers were normal. They were long and the nails were exquisitely manicured.

"That's Solum," said Havana, leaning forward over the counter and talking across the two girls. "He's the Alligator-Skinned Man, an' the ugliest human in captivity." He must have sensed Horty's thought that Solum might resent this designation, for he added, "He's deaf. He don't know what goes on."

"I'm Bunny," said the girl next to him. She was plump—not fat like Havana, but round—butter-ball round, skin-tight round. Her flesh was flesh colored and blood-colored—all pink with no yellow about it. Her hair was as white as cotton, but glossy, and her eyes were the extraordinary ruby of a white rabbit's. She had a little midge of a voice and an all but ultra-sonic giggle, which she used now. She stood barely as high as his shoulder, though they sat at the same height. She was out of proportion only in this one fact of the long torso and the short legs. "An' this is Zena."

Horty turned his gaze full on her and gulped. She was the most beautiful little work of art he had ever seen in his life. Her dark hair shone, and her eyes shone too, and her head planed from temple to cheek, curved from cheek to chin, softly and smoothly. Her skin was tanned over a deep, fresh glow like the pink shadows between the petals of a rose. The lipstick she chose was dark, nearly a brown red; that and the dark skin made the whites of her eyes like beacons. She wore a dress with a wide collar that lay back on her shoulders, and a neckline that dropped almost to her waist. That neckline told Horty for the very first time that these kids, Havana and Bunny and Zena, weren't kids at all. Bunny was girl-curved, puppy-fat curved, the way even a four-year-old girl—or boy—might be. But Zena had breasts, real, taut, firm, separate breasts. He looked at them and then at the three small faces, as if the faces he had seen before had disappeared and were replaced by new ones. Havana's studied, self-assured speech and his cigars were his badges of maturity, and albino Bunny would certainly show some such emblem in a minute.

"I won't tell you his name," said Havana. "He's fixin' to get a new one, as of now. Right, kid?"

"Well," said Horty, still struggling with the strange shifting of estimated place these people had made within him, "Well, I guess so."

"He's cute," said Bunny. "You know that, kid?" She uttered her almost inaudible giggle. "You're cute."

Horty found himself looking at Zena's breasts again and his cheeks flamed. "Don't rib him," said Zena.

It was the first time she had spoken . . . One of the earliest things Horty could remember was a cat-tail stalk he had seen lying on the bank of a tidal creek. He was only a toddler then, and the dark-brown sausage of the cat-tail fastened to its dry yellow stem had seemed a hard and brittle thing. He had, without picking it up, run his fingers down its length, and the fact that it was not dried wood, but velvet, was a thrilling shock. He had such a shock now, hearing Zena's voice for the first time.

The short-order man, a pasty-faced youth with a tired mouth and laugh-wrinkles around his eyes and nostrils, lounged up to them. He apparently felt no surprise at seeing the midgets or the hideous green-skinned Solum. "Hi, Havana. You folks setting up around here?"

"Not fer six weeks or so. We're down Eltonville way. We'll milk the State Fair and work back. Comin' in with a load o' props. Cheeseburger fer the glamor-puss there. What's yer pleasure, ladies?"

"Scrambled on rye toast," said Bunny.

Zena said, "Fry some bacon until it's almost burned—"

"—an' crumble it over some peanut-butter on whole wheat. I remember, princess," grinned the cook. "What say, Havana?"

"Steak. You too, huh?" he asked Horty. "Nup—he can't cut it. Ground sirloin, an' I'll shoot you if you bread it. Peas an' mashed."

The cook made a circle of his thumb and forefinger and went to get the order.

Horty asked, timidly, "Are you with a circus?"

"Carny," said Havana.

Zena smiled at his expression. It made his head swim. "That's a carnival. You know. Does your hand hurt?"

"Not much."

"That kills me," Havana exploded. "Y'oughta see it." He drew his right hand across his left fingers and made a motion like crumbling crackers. "Man."

"We'll get that fixed up. What are we going to call you?" asked Bunny.

"Let's figure out what he's going to do first," said Havana. "We got to make the Maneater happy."

"About those ants," said Bunny, "would you eat slugs and grasshoppers, and that?" She asked him straight out, and this time she did not giggle.

"No!" said Horty, simultaneously with Havana's "I already asked him that. That's out, Bunny. The Maneater don't like to use a geek anyway."

Regretfully, Bunny said, "No carny ever had a midge that would geek. It would be a card."

"What's a geek?" asked Horty.

"He wants to know what's a geek."

"Nothing very nice," said Zena. "It's a man who eats all sorts of nasty things, and bites the heads off live chickens and rabbits."

Horty said, "I don't think I'd like doing that," so soberly that the three midgets burst into a shrill explosion of laughter. Horty looked at them all, one by one, and sensed that they laughed with, not at him, and so he laughed too. Again he felt that inward surge of warmth. These folk made everything so easy. They seemed to understand that he could be a little different from other folks, and it was all right. Havana had apparently told them all about him, and they were eager to help.

"I told you," said Havana, "he sings like an angel. Never heard anything like it. Wait'll you hear."

"You play anything?" asked Bunny. "Zena, could you teach him guitar?"

"Not with that left hand," said Havana.

"*Stop* it!" Zena cried. "Just when did you people decide he was going to work with us?"

Havana opened his mouth helplessly. Bunny said, "Oh—I thought . . ." and Horty stared at Zena. Were they trying to give and take away all at the same time?

"Oh, kiddo, don't look at me like that," said Zena. "You'll tear me apart. . ." Again, in spite of his distress, he could all but feel her voice with fingertips. She said, "I'd do anything in the world for you, child. But—it would have to be something good. I don't know that this would be good."

"Sure it'd be good," scoffed Havana. "Where's he gonna eat? Who's gonna take him in? Listen, after what he's been through he deserves a break. What's the matter with it, Zee? The Maneater?"

"I can handle the Maneater," she said. Somehow, Horty sensed that in that casual remark was the thing about Zena that made the others await her decision. "Look, Havana," she said, "what happens to a kid his age makes him what he will be when he grows up. Carny's all right for us. It's home to us. It's the one place where we can be what we are and like it. What would it be for him, growing up in it? That's no life for a kid."

"You talk as if there was nothing in a carnival but midges and freaks."

"In a way that's so," she murmured. "I'm sorry," she added. "I shouldn't have said that. I can't think straight tonight. There's something . . ." She shook herself. "I don't know. But I don't think it's a good idea."

Bunny and Havana looked at each other. Havana shrugged helplessly. And Horty couldn't help himself. His eyes felt hot, and he said "Gee."

"Oh, Kid, don't."

"Hey!" barked Havana. "Grab him! He's fainting!"

Horty's face was suddenly pale and twisted with pain. Zena slid off her stool and put her arm around him. "Sick, honey? Your hand?"

Gasping, Horty shook his head. "Junky," he whispered, and grunted as if his windpipe were being squeezed. He pointed with his bandaged hand toward the door. "Truck," he rasped. "In—Junky—oh, truck!"

The midgets looked at one another, and then Havana leaped from his stool and, running to Solum, punched his arm. He made quick motions, pointing outside, turning an imaginary steering wheel, beckoning toward the door.

Moving with astonishing speed, the big man slipped to the door and was gone, the others following. Solum was at the truck almost before the midgets and Horty were outside. He bounded catlike past the cab, throwing a quick glance into it, and in two more jumps was at the tail gate and inside. There were a couple of thumps and Solum emerged, the tattered figure of a man dangling from his parti-colored hands. The tramp was struggling, but when the brilliant golden light fell on Solum's face, he uttered a scratchy ululation which must have been clearly audible a quarter of a mile away. Solum dropped him on to the cinders; he landed heavily on his back and lay there writing and terrified, fighting to get wind back into his shocked lungs.

Havana threw away his cigar stub and pounced on the prone figure, roughly going through the pockets. He said something unprintable and then, "Look here —our new soupspoons and four compacts and a lipstick and—why, you little sneak," he snarled at the man, who was not large but was nearly three times his size. The man twitched as if he would throw Havana off him; Solum immediately leaned down and raked a large hand across his face. The man screamed again, and this time did surge up and send Havana flying; not, however, to attack, but to run sobbing and slobbering with fear from the gaunt Solum. He disappeared into the darkness across the highway with Solum at his heels.

Horty went to the tailgate. He said, timidly, to Havana, "Would you look for my package?"

"That ol' paper bag? Sure." Havana swung up on the tailgate, reappeared a moment later with the bag, and handed it to Horty.

Armand had broken Junky very thoroughly, breaking the jack-in-the-box's head away from the rest of the toy, flattening it until all that Horty could salvage was the face. But now the ruin was complete.

"Gee," said Horty. "Junky. He's all busted." He drew out the two pieces of the hideous face. The nose was crushed to a coarse powder of papier-maché, and the face was cracked in two, a large piece and a small piece. There was an eye in each, glittering. "Gee," Horty said again, trying to fit them together with one hand.

Havana, busy gathering up the loot, said over his shoulder, " 'Sa damn shame, kid. The guy must've put his knee on it while he was goin' through our stuff." He tossed the odd collection of purchases into the cab of the truck while Horty wrapped Junky up again. "Let's go back inside. Our order'll be up."

"What about Solum?" asked Horty.

"He'll be along."

Horty was conscious, abruptly, that Zena's deep eyes were fixed on him. He almost spoke to her, didn't know what to say, flushed in embarrassment, and led the way into the restaurant. Zena sat beside him this time. She leaned across him for the salt, and whispered, "How did you know someone was in the truck?"

Horty settled his paper bag in his lap, and saw her eyes on it as he did so. "Oh," she said; and then in quite a different tone, slowly, "Oh-h." He had no answer to her question, but he knew, suddenly, that he would not need one. Not now.

"How'd you know there was someone out there?" demanded Havana, busy with a catsup bottle.

Horty began to speak, but Zena interrupted. "I've changed my mind," she said suddenly. "I think carny can do the kid more good than harm. It's better than making his way on the outside."

"Well now." Havana put down the bottle and beamed. Bunny clapped her hands. "*Good,* Zee! I knew you'd see it."

Havana added, "So did I. I . . . see somp'n else, too." He pointed.

"Coffee urn?" said Bunny stupidly. "Toaster?"

"The mirror, stoopid. Will you look?" He leaned close to Horty and put an arm around his head, drawing his and Zena's faces together. The reflections looked back at them—small faces, both brown, both deep-eyed, oval, dark-haired. If Horty were wearing lipstick and braids, his face would have been different from hers—but very little.

"Your long-lost brother!" breathed Bunny.

"My cousin—and I mean a *girl* cousin," said Zena. "Look—there are two bunks in my end of the wagon . . . stop that cackling, Bunny; I'm old enough to be his mother and besides—oh, shut up. No; this is the perfect way to do it. The Maneater never has to know who he is. It's up to you two."

"We won't say anything," said Havana.

Solum kept on eating.

Horty asked, "Who's the Maneater?"

"The boss," said Bunny. "He used to be a doctor. He'll fix up your hand."

Zena's eyes looked at something that was not in the room. "He hates people," she said. "All people."

Horty was startled. This was the first indication among these odd folk that there might be something to be afraid of. Zena, understanding, touched his arm. "Don't be afraid. His hating won't hurt you."

THEY REACHED THE CARNIVAL IN THE dark part of the morning, when the distant hills had just begun to separate themselves from the paling sky.

To Horty it was all thrilling and mysterious. Not only had he met these people, but there was also the excitement and mystery ahead, and the way of starting it, the game he must play, the lines he must never forget. And now, at dawn, the carnival itself. The wide dim street, paved with wood shavings, seemed faintly luminous between the rows of stands and bal-ly-platforms. Here a dark neon tube made ghosts of random light rays from the growing dawn; there one of the rides stretched hungry arms upward in bony silhouette. There were sounds, sleepy, restless, alien sounds; and the place smelled of damp earth, popcorn, perspiration, and sweet exotic manures.

The truck threaded its way behind the western row of midway stands and came to a stop by a long house-trailer with doors at each end.

"Home," yawned Bunny. Horty was riding in front with the girls now, and Havana had curled up in the back. "Out you get. Scoot, now; right into that door-way. The Maneater'll be asleep, and no one will see you. When you come out you'll be somebody differ-ent, and then we'll go fix your hand up."

Horty stood on the truck step, glanced around, and then arrowed to the door of the trailer and skinned inside. It was dark there. He stood clear of the door and waited for Zena to come in, close it, and draw the curtains on the small windows before turning on the lights.

The light seemed very bright. Horty found himself in a small square room. There was a tiny bunk on each side, a compact kitchenette in one corner, and what appeared to be a closet in the other.

"All right," said Zena, "take off your clothes."

"*All* of 'em?"

"Of course, all of them." She saw his startled face, and laughed. "Listen, Kiddo. I'll tell you something about us little people. Uh—how old did you say you were?"

"I'm almost nine."

"Well, I'll try. Ordinary grown-up people are very careful about seeing each other without clothes. Whether or not it makes any sense, they are that way because there's a big difference between men and women when they're grown up. More than between boys and girls. Well, a midget stays like a child, in most ways, all his life except for maybe a couple of years. So a lot of us don't let such things bother us. As for us, you and me, we might as well make up our minds right now that it's not going to make any difference. In the first place, no one but Bunny and Havana and me know you're a boy. In the second place, this little room is just too small for two people to live in if they're going to be stooping and cringing and hiding from each other because of something that doesn't matter. See?"

"I—I guess so."

She helped him out of his clothes, and he began his careful education on how to be a woman from the skin outward.

"Tell me something, Horty," she said, as she turned out a neat drawer, looking for clothes for him. "What's in the paper bag?"

"That's Junky. It's a jack-in-the-box. It was, I mean. Armand busted it—I told you. Then the man in the truck busted it more."

"Could I see?"

Worrying into a pair of her socks, he nodded toward one of the bunks. "Go ahead."

She lifted out the tattered bits of papier-mâché. "*Two* of them!" she exploded. She turned and looked at Horty as if he had turned bright purple, or sprouted rabbit's ears.

"Two!" she said again. "I thought I saw only one, there at the diner. Are they really yours? Both of them?"

"They're Junky's eyes," he explained.

"Where did Junky come from?"

"I had him before I was adopted. A policeman found me when I was a baby. I was put in a Home. I got Junky there. I guess I never had any folks."

"And Junky stayed with you—here, let me help you into that—Junky stayed with you from then on?"

"Yes. He had to."

"Why had to?"

"How do you hook this?"

Zena checked what seemed to be an impulse to push him into a corner and hold him still until she extracted the information from him. "About Junky," she said patiently.

"Oh. Well, I just had to have him near me. No, not near me. I could go a long way away as long as Junky was all right. As long as he was mine, I mean. I mean, if I didn't even see him for a year it was all right, but if somebody moved him, I knew it, and if somebody hurt him, I hurt too. See?"

"Indeed I do," said Zena surprisingly. Again Horty felt that sweet shock of delight; these people seemed to understand everything so well.

Horty said, "I used to think everybody had something like that. Something they'd be sick if they lost it, like. I never thought to ask anyone about it, even. And then Armand, he picked on me about Junky. He used to hide Junky to get me excited. Once he put him on a garbage truck. I got so sick I had to have a doctor. I kept yelling for Junky, until the doctor told Armand to get this Junky back to me or I would die. Said it was a fix something. Ation."

"A fixation. I know the routine," Zena smiled.

"Armand, he was mad, but he had to do it. So anyway he got tired of fooling with Junky, and put him in the top of the closet and forgot about him pretty much."

"You look like a regular dream-girl," said Zena admiringly. She put her hands on his shoulders and looked gravely into his eyes. "Listen to me, Horty. This is *very* important. It's about the Maneater. You're going to see him in a few minutes, and I'm going to have to tell a story—a whopper of a story. And you've got to help me. He just *has* to believe it, or you won't be able to stay with us."

"I can remember real good," said Horty anxiously. "I can remember anything I want to. Just tell me."

"All right." She closed her eyes for a moment, thinking hard. "I was an orphan," she said presently. "I went to live with my Auntie Jo. After I found out I was going to be a midget I ran away with a carnival. I was with it for a few years before the Maneater met me and I came to work for him. Now . . ." She wet her lips. "Auntie Jo married again and had two children. The first one died and you were the second. When she found out you were a midget too she began to be very mean to you. So you ran away. You worked a while in summer stock. One of the stagehands—the carpenter—took a shine to you. He caught you last night and took you into the wood shop and did a terrible thing to you—so terrible that you can't even talk about it. Understand? If he asks you about it, just cry. Have you got all that?"

"Sure," said Horty casually. "Which one is going to be my bed?"

Zena frowned. "Honey—this is *terribly* important. You've got to remember every single word I say."

"Oh, I do," said Horty. And to her obvious astonishment he reeled off everything she had said, word for word.

"My!" she said, and kissed him. He blushed. "You *are* a quick study! That's wonderful. All right then. You're nineteen years old and your name's—uh—Hortense. (That's in case you hear someone say 'Horty' some day and the Maneater sees you look around.) But everybody calls you Kiddo. All right?"

"Nineteen and Hortense and Kiddo. Uh-huh."

"Good. Gosh, honey, I'm sorry to give you so many things to think of at once! Now, this is something just between us. First of all, you must never, *never* let the Maneater know about Junky. We'll find a place for him here, and I don't want you to ever talk about him again, except to me. Promise?"

Wide eyed, Horty nodded. "Uh-huh."

"Good. And one more thing, just as important. The Maneater's going to fix your hand. Don't worry; he's a good doctor. But I want you to push every bit of old bandage, every little scrap of cotton he uses, over toward me if you can, without letting him notice it. I don't want you to leave a drop of your blood in his trailer, understand? Not a drop. I'm going to offer to clean up for him—he'll be glad; he hates to do it—and you help me as much as you can. All right?"

Horty promised. Bunny and Havana pounded just then. Horty went out first, holding his bad hand behind him, and they called him Zena, and Zena pirouetted out, laughing, while they goggled at Horty. Havana dropped his cigar and said "Hey."

"Zee, he's *beautiful!*" cried Bunny.

Zena help up a tiny forefinger. "*She's* beautiful, and don't you forget it."

"I feel awful funny," said Horty, twitching his skirt.

"Where on earth did you get that hair?"

"A couple of false braids. Like 'em?"

"And the dress?"

"Bought it and never wore it," said Zena. "It won't fit my chest expansion . . . Come on, kids. Let's go wake the Maneater."

They made their way among the wagons. "Take smaller steps," said Zena. "That's better. You remember everything?"

"Oh, sure."

"That's a good—a good girl, Kiddo. And if he should ask you a question and you don't know, just smile. Or cry. I'll be right beside you."

A long silver trailer was parked next to a tent bearing a brilliantly colored poster of a man in a top-hat. He had long pointed mustachios and zig-zags of lightning came from his eyes. Below it, in flaming letters, was the legend

## WHAT DO YOU THINK?
### Mephisto Knows.

"His name isn't Mephisto," said Bunny. "It's Monetre. He used to be a doctor before he was a carny. Everyone calls him Maneater. He don't mind."

Havana pounded on the door. "Hey, Maneater! Y'going to sleep all afternoon?"

"You're fired," growled the silver trailer.

"Okay," said Havana casually. "Come on out and see what we got."

"Not if you want to put it on the payroll," said the sleepy voice. There were movements inside. Bunny pushed Horty over near the door and waved to Zena to hide. Zena flattened against the trailer wall.

The door opened. The man who stood there was tall, cadaverous, with hollows in his cheeks and a long bluish jaw. His eyes seemed, in the early morning light, to be just inch-deep black sockets in his head. "What is it?"

Bunny pointed at Horty. "Maneater, who's that?"

"Who's that?" He peered. "Zena, of course. Good morning, Zena," he said, his tone suddenly courtly.

"Good morning," laughed Zena, dancing out from behind the door.

The Maneater stared from Zena to Horty and back. "Oh, my aching bankroll," he said. "A sister act. And if I don't hire her you'll quit. And Bunny and Havana will quit."

"A mind-reader," said Havana, nudging Horty.

"What's your name, kid sister?"

"My pa named me Hortense," recited Horty, "but everyone calls me Kiddo."

"I don't blame them," said the Maneater in a kindly voice. "I'll tell you what I'm going to do, Kiddo. I'm going to call your bluff. Get off the lot, and if the rest of you don't like it, you can go along with her. If I don't see any of you on the midway at eleven o'clock this morning, I'll know what you decided." He closed the door softly and with great firmness.

"Oh—*gee!*" said Horty.

"It's all right," grinned Havana. "He don't mean it. He fires everybody 'most every day. When he means it he pays 'em. Go get 'im, Zee."

Zena rippled her knuckles on the aluminum door. "Mister Maneater!" she sang.

"I'm counting your pay," said the voice from inside.

"Oh-oh," said Havana.

"Please. Just a minute," cried Zena.

The door opened up again. The Maneater had one hand full of money. "Well?"

Horty heard Bunny mutter, "Do good, Zee. Do good!"

Zena beckoned to Horty. He stepped forward hesitantly. "Kiddo, show him your hand."

Horty extended his ruined hand. Zena peeled off the soiled, bloody handkerchiefs one by one. The inner one was stuck fast; Horty whimpered as she disturbed it. Enough could be seen, however, to show the Maneater's trained eye that three fingers were gone completely and the rest of the hand in a bad way.

"How in creation did you do a thing like this, girl?" he barked. Horty fell back, frightened.

"Kiddo, go over there with Havana, hm?"

Horty retreated, gratefully. Zena began talking rapidly in a low voice. He could only hear part of it. "Terrible shock, Maneater. Don't remind her of it, ever . . . carpenter . . . and took her to his shop . . . when she . . . and her hand in the vise."

"No wonder I hate people," the Maneater snarled. He asked her a question.

"No," said Zena. "She got away, but her hand . . ."

"Come here, Kiddo," said the Maneater. His face was something to see. His whip of a voice seemed to issue from his nostrils which, suddenly, were not carven slits but distended, circular holes. Horty turned pale.

Havana pushed him gently. "Go on, Kiddo. He's not mad. He's sorry for you. Go *on!*"

Horty inched forward and timidly climbed the step. "Come in here."

"We'll see you," called Havana. He and Bunny turned away. As the door closed behind him and Zena, Horty looked back and saw Bunny and Havana gravely shaking hands.

"Sit down there," said the Maneater.

The inside of his trailer was surprisingly spacious. There was a bed across the front end, partially curtained. There was a neat galley, a shower, and a safe; a large table, cabinets, and more books than one would ever expect to fit into such space.

"Does it hurt?" murmured Zena.

"Not much."

"Don't you worry about that," growled the Man-eater. He put alcohol, cotton, and a hypodermic case on the table. "Tell you what I'm going to do. (Just to be different from other doctors.) I'm going to block the nerve on your whole arm. When I poke the needle into you it'll hurt, like a bee-sting. Then your arm will feel very funny, as if it were a balloon being blown up. Then I'll clean up that hand. It won't hurt."

Horty smiled up at him. There was something in this man, with his frightening changes of voice and his treacherous humor, his kindness and his cruel aura, which the boy found deeply appealing. There was a kindness like Kay's, little Kay who hadn't cared if he ate ants. And there was a cruelty like Armand Bluett's. If nothing else, the Maneater would serve as a link with the past for Horty—for a while at least. "Go ahead," said Horty.

"That's a good girl."

The Maneater bent to his work, with Zena, fascinated, looking on, deftly moving things out of his way, making things more convenient for him. So absorbed he became that if he had any further questions to ask about "Kiddo" he forgot them.

Zena cleaned up afterward.

PIERRE MONETRE HAD GRADUATED FROM
college three days before he was sixteen, and from
medical school when he was twenty-one. A man died
under his hands during a simple appendectomy,
which was not Pierre Monetre's fault.

But someone—a hospital trustee—made a slighting
reference to it. Monetre went to him to protest and
stayed to break the man's jaw. He was immediately
banned from the surgical theater, and rumor blamed

it on the appendectomy alone. Instead of proving to the world matters which he felt needed no proof, he resigned from the hospital. He then began to drink. He took his drunkenness before the world as he had taken his brilliance and his skill—front and center, and damn the comments. The comments on his brilliance and his skill had helped him. The comments on his drunkenness shut him out.

He got over the drunkenness; alcoholism is not a disease, but a symptom. There are two ways of disposing of alcoholism. One is to cure the disorder which causes it. The other is to substitute some other symptom for it. That was Pierre Monetre's way.

He chose to despise the men who had shut him out, and let himself despise the rest of humanity because it was kin to those men.

He enjoyed his disgust. He built himself a pinnacle of hatred and stood on it to sneer at the world. This gave him all the altitude he needed at the time. He starved while he did it; but since riches were of value to the world at which he sneered, he enjoyed his poverty too. For a while.

But a man with such an attitude is like a child with a whip—or a nation with battleships. For a while it is sufficient to stand in the sun, with one's power in plain sight for all to see. Soon, however, the whip must whistle and crack, the rifles must thunder, the man must take more than a stand; he must take action.

Pierre Monetre worked for a while with subversive groups. It was of no importance to him which group, or what it stood for, as long as its aim was to tear down the current structure of the majority. He did not confine this to politics, but also did what he could to introduce modern non-objective art into traditional galleries, agitated for atonal music in string quartets, poured beef-extract on the serving tables of a vegetarian restaurant, and made a score of other stupid, petty rebellions—rebellions for their own sake always, having nothing to do with the worth of any art or music or food-taboos.

His disgust, meanwhile, fed on itself, until it was neither stupid nor petty. Again he found himself at a loss for a means of expressing it. He grew increasingly bitter as his clothes wore out, as he was forced out of one sordid garret after another. He never blamed himself, but felt victimized by humanity—a humanity that was, part and parcel, inferior to him. And suddenly he was given what he wanted.

He had to eat. All his corrosive hatreds focussed there. There was no escaping it, and for a while there was no means of eating except doing work which would be of some value to some part of humanity. This galled him, but there was no other way of inducing humanity to pay him for his work. So he turned to a phase of his medical training and got a job in a biological laboratory doing cellular analyses. His hatred of mankind could not change the characteristics of his interested, inquiring, brilliant mind; he loved the work, hating only the fact that it benefited people—employers and their clients, who were mostly doctors and their patients.

He lived in a house—an ex-stable—near the edge of a small town, where he could take long walks by himself in the woods and think his strange thoughts. Only a man who had consciously turned away, for years, from everything human would have noticed what he had noticed one fall afternoon, or would have had the curiosity to examine it. Only a man with his unusual combination of training and ability would have had the equipment to explain it. And certainly, only such a social monster could have used it as he did.

He saw two trees.

Each was a tree like any other tree—an oak sapling, twisted from some early accident, young and alive. Never in a thousand years would he have noticed either of them, particularly, had he seen it alone. But he saw them together; his eye swept over them, he raised his eyebrows in slight surprise and walked on. Then he stopped and went back and stood staring at them. And suddenly he grunted as if he had been kicked, and went between the trees—they were twenty feet apart—and gaped from one to the other.

The trees were the same size. Each had a knotted primary limb snaking off to the north. Each had a curling scar on the first shoot from it. The first cluster on the primary on each tree had five leaves on it.

Monetre went and stood closer, running his gaze from tree to tree, up and down, one, then the other.

What he saw was impossible. The law of averages permits of such a thing as two absolutely identical trees, but at astronomical odds. Impossible was the working word for such a statistic.

Monetre reached and pulled down a leaf from one

tree, and from the other took down its opposite number.

They were identical—veining, shape, size, texture.

That was enough for Monetre. He grunted again, looked searchingly around to fix the location in his mind, and headed back to his shack at a dead run.

Far into the night he labored over the oak leaves. He stared through a magnifying glass until his eyes ached. He made solutions of what he had in the house —vinegar, sugar, salt, a little phenol—and marinated parts of the leaves. He dyed corresponding parts of them with diluted ink.

What he found out about them checked and double-checked when he took them to the laboratory in the morning. Qualitative and quantitative analysis, volumetric and kindling temperature and specific gravity tests, spectrographics and pH ratings—all said the same thing; these two leaves were incredibly and absolutely identical.

Feverishly, in the months that followed, Monetre worked on parts of the trees. His working microscopes told the same story; he talked his employer into letting him use the 300-power mike which the lab kept in a bell-jar, and it said the same thing. The trees were identical, not leaf for leaf, but cell for cell. Bark and cambium and heartwood, they were the same.

It was his own incessant sampling which gave him his next lead. He took his specimens from the trees after the most meticulous measurements. A core-drill "take" from Tree A was duplicated on Tree B, to the fractional millimeter. And one day Monetre positioned his drill on both trees, got his sample from Tree A, and, in removing it, broke the drill before he could obtain his specimen from the second tree.

He blamed it, of course, on the drill, and therefore on the men who made it, and therefore on all men; and he fumed home, happily in his own ground.

But when he came back the next day he found a hole in Tree B, exactly on the corresponding spot to his tap on Tree A.

He stood with his fingers on the inexplicable hole, and for a long moment his active mind was at a complete stop. Then, carefully, he took out his knife and cut a cross in Tree A, and, in the same place on Tree B, a triangle. He cut them deep and clear, and went home again to read more esoteric books on cell structure.

When he returned to the forest, he found both trees bearing a cross.

He made many more tests. He cut odd shapes in each tree. He painted swatches of color on them.

He found that overlays, like paint and nailed-on pieces of board, remained as he applied them. But anything effecting the structure of the tree—a cut or scrape or laceration or puncture—was repeated, from Tree A to Tree B.

Tree A was the original. Tree B was some sort of a . . . copy.

Pierre Monetre worked on Tree B for two years before he found out, with the aid of an electron microscope, that aside from the function of exact duplication, Tree B was different. In the nucleus of each cell of Tree B was a single giant molecule, akin to the hydrocarbon enzymes, which could transmute elements. Three cells removed from a piece of bark or leaf-tissue meant three cells replaced within an hour. The freak enzyme, depleted, would then rest for an hour or two, and slowly begin to restore itself, atom by captured atom, from the surrounding tissue.

The control of restoration in damaged tissue is a subtle business at its simplest. Any biologist can give a lucid description of what happens when cells begin to rebuild—what metabolistic factors are present, what oxygen exchange occurs, how fast and how large and for what purpose new cells are developed. But they cannot tell you *why*. They cannot say what gives the signal, "Start!" to a half-ruined cell, and what says "stop." They know that cancer is a malfunction of this control mechanism, but what the mechanism is they do not say. This is true of normal tissue.

But what of Pierre Monetre's Tree B? It never restored itself normally. It restored itself only to duplicate Tree A. Notch a twig of Tree A. Break off the corresponding twig of Tree B and take it home. For twelve to fourteen hours, that twig would work on the laborious process of reforming itself to be notched. After that it would stop, and be an ordinary piece of wood. Return then to Tree B, and you would find another restored twig, and this one with its notch perfectly duplicated.

Here even Pierre Monetre's skill bogged down. Cell regeneration is a mystery. Cell duplication is a step beyond an unfathomable enigma. But somewhere, somehow, this fantastic duplication was controlled, and Monetre doggedly set about finding what did it.

He was a savage, hearing a radio and searching for the signal source. He was a dog, hearing his master cry out in pain because a girl wrote that she did not love him. He saw the result, and he tried, without adequate tools, without the capacity to understand it if it were thrust under his nose, to determine the cause.

A fire did it for him.

The few people who knew him by sight—none knew him any other way—were astonished that he joined the volunteer fire-fighters that autumn, when the smoke blasted through the hills driven by a flame-whipped wind. And for years there was a legend about the skinny feller who fought the fire like a soul promised release from hell. They told about cutting the new fire-trail, and how the skinny feller threatened to kill the forest ranger if he did not move his fire line a hundred yards north of where it had been planned. The skinny feller made history with his battle of the back-blaze, watering it with his very sweat to keep it out of a certain patch of wood. And when the fire advanced to the edge of the back-blaze, and the men broke and fled before it, the skinny feller was not with them, but stayed, crouched in the smoking moss between two oak saplings, with a spade and an axe in his bleeding hands and a fire in his eyes hotter than any that ever touched a tree. They saw all of that—

They did not see Tree B begin to tremble. Their eyes were not with Monetre's, to peer through heat and smoke and the agonized cloud of exhaustion which hovered around him, and see the scientist's mind reaching out to seize on the fact that the shuddering of Tree B was timed exactly with the rolling flames over a clearing fifty feet away.

He watched it, red-eyed. Flame touched the rocky clearing, and the tree shivered. Flame tugged the earth like hair in a hurricane pulling a scalp, and when the fire wavered and streamed upward, Tree B stood firm. But when a tortured gust of cold air rushed in to fill the heat-born vacuum, and was pursued along the ground by fingers of fire, the tree shook and tensed, wavered and trembled.

Monetre dragged his half-flayed body to the clearing and watched the flames. A spear of red-orange there; the tree stood firm. A lick of a fiery tongue here, and the tree moved.

So he found it, in the middle of a basalt outcropping. He turned over a rock with fingers which sizzled when they touched it, and under it he found a muddy crystal. He thrust it under his armpit and staggered, tottered, back to his trees, which were now in a small island built of earth and sweat and fire by his own demonaic energy, and he collapsed between the oak saplings while the fire roared past him.

Just before dawn he staggered through a nightmare, a spitting, dying inferno, to his house, and hid the crystal. He dragged himself a quarter of a mile further toward the town before he collapsed. He regained consciousness in the hospital and immediately began demanding to be released. First they refused, next they tied him to his bed, and finally he left, at night, through the window, to be with his jewel.

Perhaps it was because he was at the ragged edge of insanity, or because the fusion between his conscious and unconscious minds was almost complete. More likely it was because he was peculiarly equipped, with that driving, searching mind of his. Certainly few, if any, men had ever done it before, but he did it. He established a contact with the jewel.

He did it with the bludgeon of his hatred. The jewel winked passively at him through all his tests—all that he dared give it. He had to be careful, once he found out that it was alive. His microscope told him that; it was not a crystal, but a supercooled liquid. It was a single cell, with a faceted wall. The solidified fluid inside was a colloid, with an index of refraction like that of polystyrene, and there was a complex nucleus which he did not understand.

His eagerness quarreled with his caution; he dared not run excessive heat, corrosion, and bombardment tests on it. Wildly frustrated, he sent to it a blast of the refined hatred which he had developed over the years, and the thing—screamed.

There was no sound. It was a pressure in his mind. There was no word, but the pressure was an agonized negation, a "no"-flavored impulse.

Pierre Monetre sat stunned at his battered table, staring out of the dark of his room at the jewel, which he had placed in the pool of light under a gooseneck lamp. He leaned forward and narrowed his eyes, and with complete honesty—for he had a ravening dislike of anything which bid to defy his understanding—he sent out the impulse again.

"*No!*"

The thing reacted, by that soundless cry, as if he had prodded it with a hot pin.

He was, of course, quite familiar with the phenomena of piezoelectricity, wherein a crystal of quartz or Rochelle salts would yield a small potential when squeezed, or would slightly change its dimensions when voltage was applied across it. Here was something analagous, for all the jewel was not a true crystal. His thought-impulse apparently brought a reaction from the jewel in thought "frequencies."

He pondered.

There was an unnatural tree, and it had been connected, in some way, with this buried jewel, fifty feet away; for when flame came near the jewel, the tree trembled. When he flicked the jewel with the flame of his hatred, it reacted.

Could the jewel have *built* that tree, with the other as a model? But how? *How?*

"Never mind how," he muttered. He'd find that out in good time. He could hurt the thing. Laws and punishment hurt; oppression hurts; power is the ability to inflict pain. This fantastic object would do what he wanted it to do or he would flog it to death.

He caught up a knife and ran outside. By the light of a waning moon he dug up a sprig of basil which grew near the old stable and planted it in a coffee can. In a similar can he put earth. Bringing them inside, he planted the jewel in the second can.

He composed himself at the table, gathering a particular strength. He had known that he had an extraordinary power over his own mind; in a way he was like a contortionist, who can make a shoulder muscle, or a thigh or part of an arm, jump and twitch individually. He did a thing like tuning an electronic instrument, with his brain. He channeled his mental energy into the specific "wave-length" which hurt the jewel, and suddenly, shockingly, spewed it out.

Again and again he struck out at the jewel. Then he let it rest while he tried to bring into the cruel psychic blows some directive command. He visualized the drooping basil shrub, picturing it in the second can.

*Grow one.*
*Copy that.*
*Make another.*
*Grow one.*

Repeatedly he slashed and slugged the jewel with the order. He could all but hear it whimper. Once he detected, deep in his mind, a kaleidoscopic flicker of impressions—the oak tree, the fire, a black, star-studded emptiness, a triangle cut into bark. It was brief, and nothing like it was repeated for a long time, but Monetre was sure that the impressions had come from the jewel; that it was protesting something.

It gave in; he could feel it surrender. He bludgeoned it twice more for good measure, and went to bed.

In the morning he had two basil plants. But one was a freak.

CARNIVAL LIFE PLODDED STEADILY
along, season holding the tail of the season before.
The years held three things for Horty. They were—
belonging; Zena; and a light with a shadow.

After the Maneater fixed up his—"her"—hand, and
the pink scar-tissue came in, the new midget was accepted. Perhaps it was the radiation of willingness,
the delighted, earnest desire to fit in and to be of real
value that did it, and perhaps it was a quirk or a care-
lessness on the Maneater's part, but Horty stayed.

In the carnival the pinheads and the roustabouts, the barkers and their shills, the dancers and fireaters and snake-men and ride mechanics, the layout and advance men, had something in common which transcended color and sex and racial and age differences. They were carny, all of them, interested in gathering their tips and turning them—which is carnivalese for collecting a crowd and persuading it to file past the ticket-taker—for this, and for this alone, they worked. And Horty was a part of it.

Horty's voice was a part of Zena's in their act, which followed Bets and Bertha, another sister team with a total poundage in the seven hundreds. Billed as The Little Sisters, Zena and Kiddo came on with a hilarious burlesque of the preceding act, and then faded to one of their own, a clever song-and-dance routine which ended in a bewildering vocal—a harmonizing yodel. Kiddo's voice was clear and true, and blended like keys on an organ with Zena's full contralto. They also worked in the Kiddie's Village, a miniature town with its own fire station, city hall, and restaurants, all child-size; adults not admitted. Kiddo served weak tea and cookies to the round-eyed, freckle-faced moppets at the country fairs, and felt part of their wonder and part of their belief in this magic town. Part of . . . part of . . . it was a deep-down, thrilling theme to everything that Kiddo did; Kiddo was part of Horty, and Horty was part of the world, for the first time in his life.

Their forty trucks wound among the Rockies and filed out along the Pennsylvania Turnpike, snorted into the Ottawa Fairgrounds and blended themselves into the Fort Worth Exposition. Once, when he was ten, Horty helped the giant Bets bring her child into the world, and thought nothing of it, since it was so much a part of the expected-unexpected of being a carny. Once a pinhead, a happy, brainless dwarf who sat gurgling and chuckling with joy in a corner of the freak show, died in Horty's arms after drinking lye, and the scar in Horty's memory of that frightening scarlet mouth and the pained and puzzled eyes—that scar was a part of Kiddo, who was Horty, who was part of the world.

And the second thing was Zena, who was hands for him, eyes for him, a brain for him until he got into the swing of things, until he learned to be, with utter naturalness, a girl midget. It was Zena who made him belong, and his starved ego soaked it up. She read to him, dozens of books, dozens of kinds of books, in that deep, expressive voice which quite automatically took the parts of all the characters in a story. She led him, with her guitar and her phonograph records, into music. Nothing he learned changed him; but nothing he learned was forgotten. For Horty-Kiddo had eidetic memory.

Havana used to say it was a pity about that hand. Zena and Kiddo wore black gloves in their act, which seemed a little odd; and besides, it would have been nice if they both played guitar. But of course that was out of the question. Sometimes Havana used to remark to Bunny, at night, that Zena was going to wear her fingers plumb off if she played all day on the bally-platform and all night to amuse Horty; for the guitar would cry and ring for hours after they bedded down. Bunny would say sleepily that Zena knew what she was doing—which was, of course, perfectly true.

She knew what she was doing when she had Huddie thrown out of the carnival. That was bad, for a while. She violated the carny's code to do it, and she was carny through and through. It wasn't easy, especially because there was no harm in Huddie. He was a roustabout, with a broad back and a wide, tender mouth. He idolized Zena, and was happy to include Kiddo in his inarticulate devotion. He brought them cookies and cheap little scatter-pins from the towns, and squatted out of sight against the base of their bally-platform to listen raptly while they rehearsed.

He came to the trailer to say goodbye when he was fired. He had shaved, and his store suit didn't fit very well. He stood on the step holding a battered straw "keyster" and chewed hard on some half-formed words that he couldn't quite force out. "I got fired," he said finally.

Zena touched his face. "Did—did the Maneater tell you why?"

Huddie shook his head. "He jus' called me in and handed me my time. I ain't done nothin', Zee. I—I didn' say nothin' t'him, though. Way he looked, he like to kill me. I—I jus' wish . . ." He blinked, set down his suitcase, and wiped his eyes on his sleeve. "Here," he said. He reached into his breast pocket, thrust a small package at Zena, turned and ran.

Horty, sitting on his bunk and listening wide-eyed, said, "Aw . . . Zee, what's he done? He's such a *nice* feller!"

Zena closed the door. She looked at the package. It was wrapped in gilt gift paper and had a red ribbon with a multiple, stringy bow. Huddie's big hands must have spent an hour over it. Zena slipped the ribbon off. Inside was a chiffon kerchief, gaudy and cheap and just the bright present that Huddie would choose after hours of careful searching.

Horty suddenly realized that Zena was crying. "What's the matter?"

She sat beside him and took his hands. "I went and told the Maneater that Huddie was—was bothering me. That's why he was fired."

"But—Huddie never did anything to you! Nothing bad."

"I know," Zena whispered. "Oh, I know. I lied. Huddie had to go—right away."

Horty stared at her. "I don't understand about that, Zee."

"I'm going to explain it to you," she said carefully. "It's going to hurt, Horty, but maybe that'll prevent something else happening that will hurt much more. Listen. You always remember everything. You were talking to Huddie yesterday, remember?"

"Oh, yes. I was watching him and Jemmy and Ole and Stinker drive stakes. I love to watch 'em. They stand around in a circle with their big heavy sledge-hammers and each one taps easy—plip, plip, plip, plip —and then each one swings the hammer right over their head and hits with all their might—blap, blap, blap, blap!—so *fast!* An' that ol' stake, it jus' *melts* into the ground!" He stopped, his eyes shining, hearing and seeing the machine-gun rhythm of the sledge crew with all the detail of his sound-camera mind.

"Yes, dear," said Zena patiently. "And what did you say to Huddie?"

"I went to feel the top of the stake inside the iron band, where it was all splintery. I said, 'my, it's all mashed!' And Huddie, he said, 'Jus' think how mashed your hand'd be iff'n you lef' it there while we-uns drove it.' And I laughed at him an' said, 'It wouldn't bother me for long, Huddie. It would grow back again.' That's all, Zee."

"None of the others heard?"

"No. They were starting the next stake."

"All right, Horty. Huddie had to go because you said that to him."

"But—but he thought it was a joke! He just laughed . . . what did I *do*, Zee?"

"Horty sweetheart, I told you that you must never say the slightest, tiniest word to anyone about your hand, or about anything growing back after it gets cut off, or anything at all like that. You've got to wear a glove on your left hand day and night, and never do a thing with—"

"—with my three new fingers?"

She clapped a hand over his mouth. "Never talk about it," she hissed, "to anyone but me. *No one* must know. Here." She rose and tossed the dazzling kerchief on his lap. "Keep this. Look at it and think about it and—and leave me alone for a while. Huddie was —I . . . I can't like you very much for a little while, Horty. I'm sorry."

She turned away from him and went out, leaving him shocked and hurt and deeply ashamed. And when, very late that night, she came to his bed and slid her warm, small arms around him and told him it was all right now, he needn't cry any more, he was so happy he could not speak. He burrowed his face into her shoulder and trembled, and he made a promise—a deep promise, to himself, not to her, that he would always, always do as she said. They never spoke of Huddie again.

Sights and smells were treasures; he treasured the books they read together—fantasies like *The Worm Ouroborus* and *The Sword in the Stone* and *The Wind in the Willows;* strange, quizzical, deeply human books, each the only one of its kind, like *Green Mansions,* Bradbury's *Martian Chronicles,* Capek's *War with the Newts,* and *The Innocent Voyage.*

Music was a treasure—laughing music like the Polka from the "Isle of Gold" and the cacaphonous ingenuities of Spike Jones and Red Ingalls; the rich romanticism of Crosby, singing "Adeste Fideles" or "Skylark" as if each were his only favorite, and Tchaikovsky's azure sonorities; and the architects, Franck building with feathers, flowers and faith, Bach with agate and chrome.

But the things Horty treasured most were the drowsy conversations in the dark, sometimes on a silent fairgrounds after hours, sometimes bumping along a moonwashed road.

"Horty—" (She was the only one who called him Horty. No one else heard her do it. It was like a private pet-name.)

"Mmm?"

"Can't you sleep?"

"Thinkin' . . ."

"Thinking about your childhood sweetheart?"

"How'd you know? Uh—don't kid me, Zee."

"Oh, I'm sorry, honey."

Horty said into the darkness, "Kay was the only one who ever said anything nice to me, Zee. The only one. It wasn't only that night I ran away. Sometimes in school she'd just smile, that's all. I—I used to wait for it. You're laughing at me."

"No, Kiddo, I'm not. You're so sweet."

"Well," he said defensively, "I like to think about her sometimes."

He did think about Kay Hallowell, and often; for this was the third thing, the light with a shadow. The shadow was Armand Bluett. He could not think of Kay without thinking of Armand, though he tried not to. But sometimes the cold wet eyes of a tattered mongrel in some farmyard, or the precise, heralding sound of a key in a Yale lock, would bring Armand and Armand's flat sarcasm and Armand's hard and ready hands right into the room with him. Zena knew of this, which is why she always laughed at him when he mentioned Kay . . .

He learned so much in those somnolent talks. About the Maneater, for example. "How'd he ever get to be a carny, Zee?"

"I can't say exactly. Sometimes I think he hates carny. He seems to despise the people who come in, and I guess he's in the business mostly because it's the only way he can keep his—" She fell silent.

"What, Zee?"

She was quiet until he spoke again. "He has some

people he—thinks a lot of," she explained at length. "Solum. Gogol, the Fish Boy. Little Pennie was one of them." Little Pennie was the pinhead who had drunk lye. "A few others. And some of the animals. The two-legged cat, and the Cyclops. He—likes to be near them. He kept some of them before he got into show business. But it must have cost a lot. This way, he can make money out of them."

"Why does he like them, 'specially?"

She turned restlessly. "He's the same kind they are," she breathed. Then, "Horty, don't *ever* show him your hand!"

One night in Wisconsin something woke Horty. *Come here.*

It wasn't a sound. It wasn't in words. It was a call. There was a cruel quality to it. Horty lay still.

*Come here, come here. Come! Come!*

Horty sat up. He heard the prairie wind, and the crickets.

*Come!* This time it was different. There was a coruscating blaze of anger in it. It was controlled and directive, and had in it a twinge of the pleasure of an Armand Bluett in catching a boy in an inarguable wrong. Horty swung out of bed and stood up, gasping.

"Horty? Horty—what is it?" Zena, naked, came sliding out of the dim whiteness of her sheets like the dream of a seal in surf.

"I'm supposed to—go," he said with difficulty.

"What is it?" she whispered tensely. "Like a voice inside you?"

He nodded. The furious command struck him again, and he twisted his face.

"Don't go," Zena whispered. "You hear me, Horty? Don't you move." She spun into a robe. "You get back into bed. Hold on tight; whatever you do, don't leave this trailer. The—it will stop. I promise you it will stop quickly." She pressed him back to his bunk. "Don't you go, now, no matter what happens."

Blinded, stunned by this urgent, painful pressure, he sank back on the bunk. The call flared again within him; he started up. "Zee—" But she was gone. He stood up, his head in his hands, and then remembered the furious urgency of her orders, and sat down again.

It came again and was—incomplete. Interrupted.

He sat quite still and felt for it with his mind, timidly, as if he were tonguing a sensitive tooth. It was gone. Exhausted, he fell back and went to sleep.

In the morning Zena was back. He had not heard her come in. When he asked her where she had been, she gave him a curious look and said, "Out." So he did not ask her anything more. But at breakfast with Bunny and Havana, she suddenly gripped his arm, taking advantage of a moment when the others had left the table to stove and toaster. "Horty! If you ever get a call like that again, wake me. Wake me right away, you hear?" She was so fierce he was frightened; he had only time to nod before the others came back. He never forgot it. And after that, there were not many times when he woke her and she slipped out, wordlessly, to come back hours later; for when he realized the calls were not for him, he no longer felt them.

The seasons passed and the carnival grew. The Maneater was still everywhere in it, flogging the roustabouts and the animal men, the daredevils and the drivers, with his weapon—his contempt, which he carried about openly like a naked sword.

The carnival grew—larger. Bunny and Havana grew—older, and so did Zena, in subtle ways. But Horty did not grow at all.

He—she—was a fixture now, with a clear soprano voice and black gloves. He passed with the Maneater, who withheld his contempt in saying "Good Morning"—a high favor—and who had little else to say. But Horty-Kiddo was loved by the rest, in the earnest, slap-dash way peculiar to carnies.

The show was a flat-car rig now, with press-agents and sky-sweeping searchlights, a dance pavilion and complicated, epicyclic rides. A national magazine had run a long picture story on the outfit, with emphasis on its "Strange People" ("Freak Show" being an unpopular phrase.) There was a press office now, and there were managers, and annual re-bookings from big organizations. There were public-address systems for the bally-platforms, and newer—not new, but newer—trailers for the personnel.

The Maneater had long since abandoned his mind-reading act, and, increasingly, was a presence only to those working on the lot. In the magazine stories, he was a "partner," if mentioned at all. He was seldom interviewed and never photographed. He spent his working hours with his staff, and stalking about the grounds, and his free time with his books and his rolling laboratory and his "Strange People." There were stories of his being found in the dark hours of the morning, standing in the breathing blackness with his hands behind him and his gaunt shoulders stooped, staring at Gogol in his tank, or peering over the two-headed snake or the hairless rabbit. Watchmen and animal men had learned to keep away from him at such times; they withdrew silently, shaking their heads, and left him alone.

"Thank you, Zena." The Maneater's tone was courtly, mellow.

Zena smiled tiredly, closed the door of the trailer against the blackness outside. She crossed to the chrome and plastic-web chair by his desk and curled up with her robe tucked over her toes. "I've had enough sleep," she said.

He poured wine—shimmering Moselle. "An odd hour for it," he offered, "but I know you like it."

She took the glass and set it on the corner of the desk. She waited. She had learned to wait.

"I found some new ones today," said the Maneater. He opened a heavy mahogany box and lifted a velvet tray out of it. "Mostly young ones."

"That's good," said Zena.

"It is and it isn't," said Monetre irascibly. "They're easier to handle—but they can't do as much. Sometimes I wonder why I bother."

"So do I," said Zena.

She thought his eyes moved to her and away in

their deep sockets, but she couldn't be sure. He said, "Look at these."

She took the tray on her lap. There were eight crystals lying on the velvet, gleaming dully. They had been freshly cleaned of the layer of dust, like dried mud, that always covered them when they were found—the layer that made them look like clods, like stones. They were not quite translucent, yet the nucleus could be seen by one who knew just what internal hovering shadow to look for.

Zena picked one up and held it to the light. Monetre grunted, and she met his gaze.

"I was wondering which one you would pick up first," he said. "That one's very alive." He took it from her and stared at it, narrowing his eyes. The bolt of hatred he aimed at it made Zena whimper. "Please don't . . ."

"Sorry . . . but it screams so," he said softly, and put it back with the others. "If I could only understand how they think," he said. "I can hurt them. I can direct them. But I can't talk to them. But some day I'll find out . . ."

"Of course," said Zena, watching his face. Was he going to have another of his furies? He was due for one . . .

He slumped into his chair, put his clasped hands between his knees and stretched. She could hear his shoulders crackle. "They dream," he said, his organ voice dwindling to an intense whisper. "That's as close to describing them as I've come yet. They dream."

Zena waited.

"But their dreams live in our world—in our kind of reality. Their dreams are not thoughts and shadows, pictures and sounds like ours. They dream in flesh and sap, wood and bone and blood. And sometimes their dreams aren't finished, and so I have a cat with two legs, and a hairless squirrel, and Gogol, who should be a man, but who has no arms, no sweat glands, no brain. They're not finished . . . they all lack formic acid and niacin, among other things. But —they're alive."

"And you don't know—yet—how the crystals do it."

He looked up at her without moving his head, so that she saw his eyes glint through his heavy brows. "I hate you," he said, and grinned. "I hate you because I have to depend on you—because I have to talk to you. But sometimes I like what you do. I like what you said—*yet*. I don't know how the crystals do their dreaming—*yet*."

He leaped to his feet, the chair crashing against the wall as he moved. "Who understands a dream fulfilled?" he yelled. Then, quietly, as if there were no excitement in him, he continued evenly, "Talk to a bird and ask it to understand that a thousand-foot tower is a man's finished dream, or that an artist's sketch is part of one. Explain to a caterpillar the structure of a symphony—and the dream that based it. Damn structure! Damn ways and means!" His fist crashed down on the desk. Zena quietly picked up her wine glass. "How this thing happens isn't important. Why it happens isn't important. But it *does* happen, and I can control it." He sat down and said to Zena, courteously, "More wine?"

"Thank you, no. I still—"

"The crystals are alive," Monetre said conversationally. "They think. They think in ways which are utterly alien to ours. They've been on this earth for hundreds, thousands of years . . . clods, pebbles, shards of stone . . . thinking their thoughts in their own way . . . striving for nothing mankind wants, taking nothing mankind needs . . . intruding nowhere, communing only with their own kind. But they have a power that no man has ever dreamed of before. And I want it. I want it. I want it, and I mean to have it."

He sipped his wine and stared into it. "They breed," he said. "They die. And they do a thing I don't understand. They die in pairs, and I throw them away. But some day I'll force them to give me what I want. I'll make a perfect thing—a man, or a woman . . . one who can communicate with the crystals . . . one who will do what I want done."

"How do—how can you be sure?" Zena asked carefully.

"Little things I get from them when I hurt them. Flashes, splinters of thought. For years I've been prodding them, and for every thousand blows I give them, I get a fragment. I can't put it into words; it's a thing I *know*. Not in detail, not quite clearly . . . but there's something special about the dream that gets *finished*. It doesn't turn out like Gogol, or like Solum—incomplete or wrongly made. It's more like that tree I found. And that finished thing will probably be human, or near it . . . and if it is, I can control it."

"I wrote an article about the crystals once," he said after a time. He began to unlock the deep lower desk drawer. "I sold it to a magazine—one of those veddy lit'ry quarterly reviews. The article was pure conjecture, to all intents and purposes. I described these crystals in every way except to say what they look like. I demonstrated the possibility of other, alien life-forms on earth, and how they could live and grow all around us without our knowledge—*provided they didn't compete*. Ants compete with humans, and weeds do, and amoebae. These crystals do not—they simply live out their own lives. They may have a group consciousness like humans—but if they do, they don't use it for survival. And the only evidence mankind has of them is their dreams—their meaningless, unfinished attempts to copy living things around them. And what do you suppose was the learned refutation stimulated by my article?"

Zena waited.

"One," said Monetre with a frightening softness, "countered with a flat statement that in the asteroid belt between Mars and Jupiter there is a body the size of a basketball which is made of chocolate cake. That, he said, is a statement which must stand as a truth because it cannot be scientifically disproved. *Damn* him!" he roared, and then went on, as softly as before, "Another explained away every evidence of malformed creatures by talking eclectic twaddle about fruit-flies, x-rays, and mutation. It's that blind, stubborn, damnable attitude that brought such masses of evidence to prove that planes wouldn't fly (for if ships needed power to keep them afloat as well as to drive them, we'd have no ships) or that trains were impractical (because the weight of the cars on the tracks would overcome the friction of the loco-motives' wheels, and the train would never start.) Volumes of logical, observer's proof showed the world was flat. Mutations? Of course there are natural muta-tions. But why must one answer be the only answer? Hard radiation mutations—demonstrable. Purely bio-chemical mutations—very probable. And the crystals' dreams . . ."

From the deep drawer he drew a labelled crystal. He took his silver cigarette lighter from the desk, thumbed it alight, and stroked the yellow flame across the crystal.

Out of the blackness came a faint, agonized scream.

"Please don't," said Zena.

He looked sharply at her drawn face. "That's Mop-pet," he said. "Have you now bestowed your affec-tions on a two-legged cat, Zena?"

"You didn't have to hurt her."

"Have to?" He brushed the crystal with the flame again, and again the scream drifted to them from the animal tent. "I had to develop my point." He snapped the lighter out, and Zena visibly relaxed. Monetre dropped lighter and crystal on the desk and went on calmly, "Evidence. I could bring that fool with his celestial chocolate cake here to this trailer, and show him what I just showed you, and he'd tell me the cat was having a stomach ache. I could show him elec-tron photomicrographs of a giant molecule inside that cat's red corpuscles actually transmuting elements—and he'd accuse me of doctoring the films. Humanity has been accursed for all its history by its insistence that what it already knows must be right, and all that differs from that must be wrong. I add my curse to the curse of history, with all my heart. Zena . . ."

"Yes, Maneater." His abrupt change in tone startled her; she had never gotten used to it.

"The complex things—mammals, birds, plants—the crystals only duplicate them if they want to—or if I flog them half to death. But some things are easy."

He rose, and drew drapes aside from the shelves behind and above him. He lifted down a rack on which was a row of chemist's watch-glasses. Setting it under the light, he touched the glass covers fondly. "Cultures," he said, in a lover's voice. "Simple, harmless ones, now. Rod bacilli in this one, and spirilla here. The *cocci* are coming along slowly, but coming for all that. I'll plant glanders, Zena, if I like, or the plague. I'll carry nuisance-value epidemics up and down this country—or wipe out whole cities. All I need to be sure of it is that middle-man—that fulfilled dream of the crystals that can teach me how they think. I'll find that middle-man, Zee, or make one. And when I do, I'll do what I like with mankind, in my own time, in my own way."

She looked up at his dark face and said nothing.

"Why do you come here and listen to me, Zena?"

"Because you call. Because you'll hurt me if I don't," she said candidly. Then, "Why do you talk to me?"

Suddenly, he laughed. "You never asked me that before, in all these years. Zena, thoughts are formless, coded . . . impulses without shape or substance or direction—until you convey them to someone else. Then they precipitate, and become ideas that you can put out on the table and examine. You don't know what you think until you tell someone else about it. That's why I talk to you. That's what you're *for*. You didn't drink your wine."

"I'm sorry." Dutifully, she drank it, looking at him wide-eyed over the rim of the glass that was too big to be her glass.

After that he let her go.

The seasons passed and there were other changes. Zena very seldom read aloud any more. She heard music or played her guitar, or busied herself with costumes and continuities, quietly, while Horty sprawled on his bunk, one hand cupping his chin, the other flipping pages. His eyes moved perhaps four times to scan each page, and their turning was a rhythmic susurrus. The books were Zena's choice, and now they were almost all quite beyond her. Horty swept the books of knowledge, breathed it in, stored it, filed it. She used to look at him, sometimes, in deep astonishment, amazed that he was Horty . . . he was Kiddo, a girl-child, who, in a few minutes would be on the bally-platform singing the "Yodelin' Jive" with her. He was Kiddo, who giggled at Cajun Jack's horseplay in the cook-tent and helped Lorelei with her brief equestrienne costumes. Yet, still giggling, or still chattering about bras and sequins, Kiddo was Horty, who would pick up a romantic novel with a bosomy dustjacket, and immerse himself in the esoteric matter it concealed—texts disguised under the false covers—

books on microbiology, genetics, cancer, dietetics, morphology, endocrinology. He never discussed what he read, never, apparently, evaluated it. He simply stored it—every page, every diagram, every word of every book she brought him. He helped her put the false covers on them, and he helped her secretly dispose of the books when he had read them—he never needed them for reference—and he never questioned her once about why he was doing it.

Human affairs refuse to be simple . . . human goals refuse to be clear. Zena's task was a dedication, yet her aims were speckled and splotched with surmise and ignorance, and the burden was heavy . . .

The rain drove viciously against the trailer in one morning's dark hours, and there was an October chill in the August air. The rain spattered and hissed like the churning turmoil she sensed so often in the Man-eater's mind. Around her was the carnival. It was around her memories too, for more years than she liked to count. The carnival was a world, a good world, but it exacted a bitter payment for giving her a place to belong. The very fact that she belonged meant a stream of goggling eyes and pointing fingers: *You're different. You're different.*

*Freak!*

She turned restlessly. Movies and love-songs, novels and plays . . . here was a woman—they called her dainty, too—who could cross a room in five strides instead of fifteen, who could envelop a doorknob in one *small* hand. She stepped up into trains instead of clambering like a little animal, and used restaurant forks without having to distort her mouth.

And they were loved, these women. They were loved, and they had choice. Their problems of choice were subtle ones, easy ones—differences between men which were so insignificant they really couldn't matter. They didn't have to look at a man and think first, first of all before anything else, *What will it mean to him that I'm a freak?*

She was little, little in so many ways. Little and stupid. The one thing she had been able to love, she had put into deadly jeopardy. She had done what she could, but there was no way of knowing if it was right.

She began to cry, silently.

Horty couldn't have heard her, but he was there. He slid into bed beside her. She gasped, and for a moment could not release her breath from her pounding throat. Then she took his shoulders, turned him away from her. She pressed her breasts against his warm back, crossed her arms over his chest. She drew him close, close, until she heard breath hissing from his nostrils. They lay still, curled, nested together like two spoons.

"Don't move, Horty. Don't say anything."

They were quiet for a long time.

She wanted to talk. She wanted to tell him of her loneliness, her hunger. Four times she pursed her lips to speak, and could not, and tears wet his shoulder instead. He lay quiet, warm and with her—just a child, but so much *with* her.

She dried his shoulder with the sheet, and put her arms around him again. And gradually, the violence of her feeling left her, and the all but cruel pressure of her arms relaxed.

At last she said two things that seemed to mean the pressures she felt. For her swollen breasts, her aching loins, she said, "I love you, Horty. I love you."

And later, for her hunger, she said, "I wish I was big, Horty. I want to be big . . ."

Then she was free to release him, to turn over, to sleep. When she awoke in the dripping half-light, she was alone.

He had not spoken, he had not moved. But he had given her more than any human being had ever given her in her whole life.

"ZEE . . ."

"Mmm?"

"Had a talk with the Maneater today while they were setting up our tent."

"What'd he say?"

"Just small-talk. He said the rubes like our act. Guess that's as near as he can get to saying he likes it himself."

"He doesn't," said Zena with certainty. "Anything else?"

"Well—no, Zee. Nothing."

"Horty, darling. You just don't know how to lie."

He laughed. "Well, it'll be all right, Zee."

There was a silence. Then, "I think you'd better tell me, Horty."

"Don't you think I can handle it?"

She turned over to face him across the trailer. "No."

She waited. Although it was pitch black, she knew Horty was biting his lower lip, tossing his head.

"He asked to see my hand."

She sat bolt upright in her bunk. "He didn't!"

"I told him it didn't give me any trouble. Gosh—when was it that he fixed it? Nine years ago? Ten?"

"Did you show it to him?"

"Cool down, Zee! No, I didn't. I said I had to fix some costumes, and got away. But he called after me and said to come to his lab before ten tomorrow. I'm just trying to think of some way to duck it."

"I was afraid of this," she said, her voice shaking. She put her arms around her knees, resting her chin on them.

"It'll be all right, Zee," said Horty sleepily. "I'll think of something. Maybe he'll forget."

"He won't forget. He has a mind like an adding machine. He won't attach any importance to it until you don't show up; then, look out!"

"Well, s'pose I do show it to him."

"I've told you and told you, Horty, you must *never* do that!"

"All right, all right.—Why?"

"Don't you trust me?"

"You know I do."

She did not answer, but sat rigidly, in thought. Horty dozed off.

Later—probably two hours later—he was awakened by Zena's hand on his shoulder. She was crouched on the floor by his bunk. "Wake up, Horty. Wake up!"

"Wuh?"

"Listen to me, Horty. You remember all you've told me—*please* wake up!—remember, about Kay, and all?"

"Oh, sure."

"What was it you were going to do, some day?"

"You mean about going back there and seeing Kay again, and getting even with that old Armand?"

"That's right. Well, that's exactly what you're going to do."

"Well, sure." He yawned and closed his eyes. She shook him again. "I mean now, Horty. Tonight. Right now."

"Tonight? Right now?"

"Get up, Horty. Get dressed. I mean it."

He sat up blearily. "Zee . . . it's night time!"

"Get dressed," she said between her teeth. "Hop to it, Kiddo. You can't be a baby all your life."

He sat on the edge of the bed and shivered away the last smoky edges of sleep. "Zee!" he cried. "Go away? You mean, leave here? Leave the carnival and Havana and—and you?"

"That's right. Get dressed, Horty."

"But—where will I go?" He reached for his clothes. "What will I do? I don't know anybody out there!"

"You know where we are? It's only fifty miles to the town you came from. That's as near as we'll get this year. Anyway, you've been here too long," she added, her voice suddenly gentle. "You should have left before—a year ago, two years, maybe." She handed him a clean blouse.

"But why do I have to?" he asked pitiably.

"Call it a hunch, though it isn't really. You wouldn't get through that appointment with the Maneater tomorrow. You've got to get out of here and stay out."

"I can't go!" he said, childishly protesting even as he obeyed her. "What are you going to tell the Maneater?"

"You had a telegram from your cousin, or some such thing. Leave it to me. You won't ever have to worry about it."

"Not ever—can't I ever come back?"

"If you ever see the Maneater again, you turn and run. Hide. Do anything, but never let him near you as long as you live."

"What about you, Zee? I'll never see you again!" He zipped up the side of a grey pleated skirt and held still for Zee's deft application of eyebrow pencil.

"Yes you will," she said softly. "Some day. Some way. Write to me and tell me where you are."

"Write to you? Suppose the Maneater should get my letter? Would that be all right?"

"It would not." She sat down, casting a woman's absent, accurate appraisal over Horty. "Write to Havana. A penny postcard. Don't sign it. Pick it out on a typewriter. Advertise something—hats or haircuts, or some such. Put your return address on it but transpose each pair of numbers. Will you remember that?"

"I'll remember," said Horty vaguely.

"I know you will. You never forget anything. You know what you're going to learn now, Horty?"

"What?"

"You're going to learn to *use* what you know. You're just a child now. If you were anyone else, I'd say you were a case of arrested development. But all the books we've read and studied . . . you remember your anatomy, Horty? And the physiology?"

"Sure, and the science and history and music and all that. Zee, what am I going to do out there? I got nobody to tell me anything!"

"You'll have to tell yourself now."

"I don't know what to do *first!*" he wailed.

"Honey, honey . . ." She came to him and kissed his forehead and the tip of his nose. "You walk out to the highway, see? And stay out of sight. Go down the road about a quarter of a mile and flag a bus. Don't ride in anything else but a bus. When you get to town wait at the station until about nine o'clock in the morning and then find yourself a room in a rooming house. A quiet one on a small street. Don't spend too much money. Get yourself a job as soon as you can. You better be a boy, so the Maneater won't know where to look."

"Am I going to grow?" he asked, voicing the professional fear of all midgets.

"Maybe. That depends. Don't go looking for Kay and that Armand creature until you're ready for it."

"How will I know when I'm ready?"

"You'll know. Got your bankbook? Keep on banking by mail, the way you always have. Got enough money? Good. You'll be all right, Horty. Don't ask anyone for anything. Don't tell anyone anything. Do things for yourself, or do without."

"I don't—belong out there," he muttered.

"I know. You will, though; just the way you came to belong here. You'll see."

Moving gracefully and easily on high heels, Horty went to the door. "Well, good-by, Zee. I—I wish I— Couldn't you come with me?"

She shook her glossy dark head. "I wouldn't dare, Kiddo. I'm the only human being the Maneater talks to—really talks to. And I've—got to watch what he's doing."

"Oh." He never asked what he should not ask. Childish, helpless, implicitly obedient, the exact, functional product of his environment, he gave her a frightened smile and turned to the door. "Good bye, honey," she whispered, smiling.

When he had gone she sank down on his bunk and cried. She cried all night. It was not until the next morning that she remembered Junky's jewelled eyes.

A DOZEN YEARS HAD PASSED SINCE KAY Hallowell had seen, from the back window, Horty Bluett climb into a brilliantly painted truck, one misty night. Those years had not treated the Hallowells kindly. They had moved into a smaller house, and then into an apartment, where her mother died. Her father had hung on for a while longer, and then had joined his wife, and Kay, at nineteen, left college in her junior year and went to work to help her brother through pre-medical school.

She was a cool blonde, careful and steady, with eyes like twilight. She carried a great deal on her shoulders, and she kept them squared. Inwardly she was afraid to be frightened, afraid to be impressionable, to be swayed, to be moved, so that outwardly she wore carefully constructed poise. She had a job to do; she had to get ahead herself so that she could help Bobby through the arduous process of becoming a doctor. She had to keep her self-respect, which meant decent housing and decent clothes. Maybe some day she could relax and have fun, but not now. Not tomorrow or next week. Just some day. Now, when she went out to dance, or to a show, she could only enjoy herself cautiously, up to the point where late hours, or a strong new interest, or even enjoyment itself, might interfere with her job. And this was a great pity, for she had a deep and brimming reservoir of laughter.

"Good morning, Judge." How she hated that man, with his twitching nostrils and his limp white hands. Her boss, T. Spinney Hartford, of Benson, Hartford and Hartford, was a nice enough man but he certainly hobnobbed with some specimens. Oh well; that's the law business. "Mr. Hartford will be with you in a moment. Please sit down, Judge."

Not there, Wet-Eyes! Oh dear, right next to her desk. Well, he always did.

She flashed him a meaningless smile and went to the filing cabinets across the room before he could start that part weak, part bewildering line of his. She hated the waste of time; there was nothing she needed from the files. But she couldn't sit there and ignore him, and she knew he wouldn't shout across the office at her; he preferred the technique described by Thorne Smith as "a voice as low as his intentions."

She felt his moist gaze on her back, on her hips, rolling up and down the seams of her stockings, and she had an attack of gooseflesh that all but itched. This wouldn't do. Maybe short range would be better; perhaps she could parry what she couldn't screen. She returned to her desk, gave him the same lipped smile, and pulled out her typewriter, swinging it up on its smooth countersprung swivels. She ran in some letterhead and began to type busily.

"Miss Hallowell."

She typed.

"Miss Hallowell." He reached and took her wrist. "Please don't be so very busy. We have such a brief moment together."

She let her hands fall into her lap—one of them, at least. She let the other hang unresisting in the Judge's limp white clasp until he let it go. She folded her hands and looked at them. That voice! If she looked up she was sure she would see a trickle of drool on his chin. "Yes, Judge?"

"Do you enjoy it here?"

"Yes. Mr. Hartford is very kind."

"A most agreeable man. Most agreeable." He waited until Kay felt so stupid, sitting there staring at her hands, that she had to raise her face. Then he said, "You plan to stay here for quite a while, then."

"I don't see why—that is, I'd like to."

"The best-laid plans . . ." he murmured. Now,

what was that? A threat to her job? What did this slavering stuffed-shirt have to do with her job? *"Mr. Hartford is a most agreeable man."* Oh. Oh dear. Mr. Hartford was a lawyer, and frequently had cases in Surrogate. Some of those were hairline decisions on which a lot depended. *"Most agreeable."* Of course Mr. Hartford was an agreeable man. He had a living to make.

Kay waited for the next gambit. It came.

"You really won't have to work here more than two more years, as I understand it."

"Wh—why? Oh. How did you know about that?"

"My dear girl," he said, with an insipid modesty. "I naturally know the contents of my own files. Your father was most provident, and very wise. When you are twenty-one, you'll be in for a comfortable bit of money, eh?"

It's none of your business, you old lynx. "Why, I'll hardly notice that, Judge. That's earmarked for Bobby, my brother. It will put him through his last two years and a year of specialization too, if he wants it. And we won't have to lose a wink of sleep over anything from then on. We're just keeping above water until then. But I'll go on working."

"Admirable." He twitched his nostrils at her, and she bit her lip and looked down at her hands again. "Very lovely," he added appreciatively. Again she waited. Move Three took place. He sighed. "Did you know there was a lien on your father's estate, for an old partnership matter?"

"I—had heard that. The old agreements were torn

up when the partnership was dissolved in Daddy's trucking business."

"One set of papers were not torn up. I still have them. Your father was a trusting man."

"That account was squared twice over, Judge!" Kay's eyes could, sometimes, take on the slate color of thunderclouds. They did now.

The Judge leaned back and put his fingertips together. "It is a matter which could get to court. To Surrogate, by the way."

He could get her job. Maybe he could get the money and with it, Bobby's career. The alternative . . . well, she could expect that now.

She was so right.

"Since my dear wife departed—" (She remembered his dear wife. A cruel, empty-headed creature with wit enough to cater to his ego in the days before he became a judge, and nothing else) "—I am a very lonely man, Miss Hallowell. I have never met anyone quite like you. You have beauty, and you could be clever. You can go far. I would like to know you better," he simpered.

Over my dead body. "You would?" she said inanely, stiff with disgust and fear.

He underlined it. "A lovely girl like you, with such a nice job, and with that little nest-egg coming to you—if nothing happens." He leaned forward. "I'm going to call you Kay from now on. I'm sure we understand each other."

"No!" She said it because she did understand, not because she didn't.

He took it his way. "Then I'd be happy to explain further," he chuckled. "Say tonight. Quite late tonight. A man in my position can't—haw!—trip the light fantastic where the lights are bright."

Kay said nothing.

"There's a little place," sniggered the Judge, "called Club Nemo, on Oak Street. Know it?"

"I think I have—noticed it," she said with difficulty.

"One o'clock," he said cheerfully. He stood up and leaned over her. He smelled like soured after-shave. "I do not like to stay up late for nothing. I'm sure you'll be there."

Her thoughts raced. She was furious, and she was frightened, two emotions which she had avoided for years. She wanted to do several things. She wanted primarily to scream, and to get rid of her breakfast then and there. She wanted to tell him some things about himself. She wanted to storm into Mr. Hartford's office and demand to know if this, this, and that were included in her duties as a stenographer.

But then, there was Bobby, so close to a career. She knew what it was to have to quit on the homestretch. And poor, fretting, worried Mr. Hartford; he meant no harm, but he wouldn't know how to handle a thing like this. And one more thing, a thing the Judge apparently did not suspect—her proven ability to land on her feet.

So instead of doing any of the things she wanted to do, she smiled timidly and said, "We'll see . . ."

"We'll see each other," he amended. "We'll see a great deal of each other." She felt that moist gaze again on the nape of her neck as he moved off, felt it on her armpits.

A light on her switchboard glowed. "Mr. Hartford will see you now, Judge Bluett," she said.

He pinched her cheek. "You can call me Armand," he whispered. "When we're alone, of course."

HE WAS THERE WHEN SHE ARRIVED. SHE was late—only a few minutes, but they cost a great deal. They were minutes added to the hours of fuming hatred, of disgust, and of fear which she had gone through after the Judge's simpering departure from the Hartford offices that morning.

She stood for a moment just inside the club. It was quiet—quiet lights, quiet colors, quiet music from a three-piece orchestra. There were very few customers, and one she knew. She caught a glimpse of silver hair in the corner back of the jutting corner of the bandstand at a shadowed table. She went to it more because she knew he would choose such a spot than because she recognized him.

He stood up and pulled out a chair for her. "I knew you'd come."

How could I get out of it, you toad? "Of course I came," she said. "I'm sorry you had to wait."

"I'm glad you're sorry. I'd have to make you sorry, if you weren't." He laughed when he said it, and only served to stress the pleasure he felt at the thought. He ran the back of his hand over her forearm, leaving a new spoor of gooseflesh. "Kay. Pretty little Kay," he moaned. "I've got to tell you something. I really put some pressure on you this morning."

You don't say! "You did?" she asked.

"You must have realized it. Well, I want you to know right away, right now, that I didn't mean any of that—except about how lonely I am. People don't realize that as well as being a judge, I'm a man."

That makes me one of the people. She smiled at him. This was a rather complicated process. It involved the fact that in this persuasive, self-pitying speech his voice had acquired a whine, and his features the down-drawn character of a spaniel's face. She half-closed her eyes to blur his image, and got such a startling facsimile of a mournful hound's head over his wing collar that she was reminded of an overheard remark: "He's that way through having been annoyed, at an early age, by the constant barking of his mother." Hence the smile. He misunderstood it and the look that went with it and stroked her arm again. Her smile vanished, though she still showed her teeth.

"What I mean is," he crooned, "I just want you to like me for myself. I'm sorry I had to use any pressure. It's just that I didn't want to fail. Anyway, all's fair . . . you know."

"—in love and war," she said dutifully. And this means war. Love me for myself alone, or else.

"I won't ask much of you," he said out of wet lips. "It's only that a man wants to feel cherished."

She closed her eyes so he could not see them roll heavenward. He wouldn't ask much. Just sneaking and skulking to protect his "position" in the town. Just that face, that voice, those hands . . . the swine, the blackmailer, the doddering, slimy-fingered old *wolf! Bobby, Bobby,* she thought in anguish, *be a* good *doctor . . .*

There was more of it, much more. A drink arrived. His choice for a sweet young girl. A sherry flip. It was too sweet and the foam on it grabbed unpleasantly at her lipstick. She sipped and let the Judge's sentimental slop wash over her, nodded and smiled, and, as often as she could, tuned out the sound of his voice and listened to the music. It was competent and clean —Hammond Solovox, string bass, and guitar—and for a while it was the only thing in the whole foul world she could hold on to.

Judge Bluett had, it seemed, a little place tucked away over a store in the slums. "The Judge works in the court and his chambers," he intoned, "and has a fine residence on The Hill. But Bluett the Man has a place too, a comfortable spot, a diamond in a rough setting, a place where he can cast aside the black robes, his dignities and his honors, and learn again that he has red blood in his veins."

"It must be very nice," she said.

"One can hide there," he said expansively. "I should say, *two* can hide there. All the conveniences. A cellar at your elbow, a larder at your beck and call. A civilized wilderness for a loaf of bread, a jug of wine, and —th-h-owoo." He ended with a hoarse whisper, and Kay had the insane feeling that if his eyes protruded another inch, a man could sit on one and saw the other off.

She closed her eyes again and explored her resources. She felt that she had possibly twenty seconds of endurance left. Eighteen. Sixteen. Oh, this is fine. Here goes Bobby's career up in smoke—in a mushroom-shaped cloud at a table for two.

He gathered his feet under him and rose. "You'll excuse me for a moment," he said, not quite clicking his heels. He made a little joke about powder rooms, and obviously being human. He turned away and turned back and pointed out that this was only the first of the little intimacies they would come to learn of each other. He turned away and turned back and said "Think it over. Perhaps we can slip away to our little dreamland this very night!" He turned away and if he had turned back again he would have gotten a French heel in the area of his watchpocket.

Kay sat alone at the table and visibly wilted. Anger and scorn had sustained her; now, for a moment, fear and weariness took their places. Her shoulders sagged and turned forward and her chin went down, and a tear slid out onto her cheek. This was three degrees worse than awful. This was too much to pay for a Mayo Clinic full of doctors. She wanted out. Something had to happen, right now.

Something did. A pair of hands appeared on the tablecloth in front of her.

She looked up and met the eyes of the young man who stood there. He had a broad, unremarkable face. He was nearly as blond as she, though his eyes were dark. He had a good mouth. He said, "A lot of people don't know the difference between a musician and a potted palm when they go to pour their hearts out. You're in a spot, Ma'am."

Some of her anger returned, but it subsided, engulfed in a flood of embarrassment. She could say only, "Please leave me alone."

"I can't. I heard that routine." He tossed his head toward the rest rooms. "There's a way out, if you'll trust me."

"I'll keep the devil I know," she said coldly.

"You listen to me. I mean listen, until I'm finished. Then you can do as you like. When he comes back, stall him off for tonight. Promise to meet him here tomorrow night. Make it a real good act. Then tell him you shouldn't leave here together; you might be seen. He'll think of that anyway."

"And he leaves, and I'm at your tender mercies?"

"Don't be a goon! Sorry. No, you leave first. Go straight to the station and catch the first train out. There's a northbound at three o'clock and a south-

bound at three-twelve. Take either one. Go somewhere else, hole up, find yourself another job, and
stay out of sight."

"On what? Three dollars mad-money?"

He flipped a long wallet out of his inside jacket
pocket. "Here's three hundred. You're smart enough
to make out all right on that."

"You're crazy! You don't know me, and I don't
know you. Besides, I haven't anything up for sale."

He made an exasperated gesture. "Who said anything about that? I said take a train—any train. No
one's going to follow you."

"You *are* crazy. How could I get it back to you?"

"You worry about that. I work here. Drop by some
time—during the day when I'm not here, if you like,
and leave it for me."

"What on earth makes you want to do a thing like
that?"

His voice was very gentle. "Say it's the same thing
makes me bring raw fish to alley-cats. Oh, stop ar-
guing. You need an out and this is it."

"I can't do a thing like that!"

"You got a good imagination? The kind that makes
pictures?"

"I—suppose so."

"Then, forgive me, but you need a kick in the teeth.
If you don't do what I just told you, that crumb is
going to—" and in a half-dozen simple, terse words, he
told her exactly what that crumb was going to do.
Then, with a single deft motion, he slipped the bills
into her handbag and got back on the bandstand.

She sat, sick and shaken, until Bluett returned from

the men's room. She had an unusually vivid pictorial imagination.

"While I was gone" he said, settling into his chair and beckoning to the waiter for the check, "know what I was doing?"

That, she thought, is just the kind of question I need right now. Limpidly, she asked, "What?"

"I was thinking about that little place, and how wonderful it would be if I could slip away after a hard day at court, and find you there waiting for me." He smiled fatuously. "And no one would ever know."

Kay sent up a "Lord-forgive-me, I-know-not-what-I-do," and said distinctly, "I think that's a charming idea. Just charming."

"And it wouldn't—*what?*"

For a moment she almost pitied him. Here he had his lines flaked out, his hooks sharpened and greased, and his casting arm worked up to a fine snap, and she'd robbed him of his sport. She'd driven up behind him with a wagon-load of fish. She'd surrendered.

"Well," he said. "Well, I, hm. Hm-m-m! Waiter!"

"But," she said archly, "Not tonight, Ar-mand."

"Now, Kay. Just come up and look at it. It's not far."

She figuratively spit on her hands, took a deep breath and plunged—wondering vaguely at just what instant she had decided to take this fantastic course. She batted her eyelashes only a delicate twice, and said softly, "Ar-mand, I'm not an experienced person like you, and I—" she hesitated and dropped her eyes— "I want it to be perfect. And tonight, it's all so sudden, and I haven't been able to look forward to anything, and it's terribly late and we're both tired, and I have to work tomorrow but I won't the day after, and besides—" and here she capped it. Here she generated, on the spot, the most diffuse and colorful statement of her entire life— "Besides," she said, fluttering her hands prettily, "I'm not *ready*."

She peeped at him from the sides of her eyes and saw his bony face undergo four distinct expressions, one after the other. Again there was that within her which was capable of astonishment; she had been able to think of only three possible reactions to a statement like that. At the same moment the guitarist behind her, in the middle of a fluid *glissando,* got his little finger trapped underneath his A string.

Before Armand Bluett could get his breath back, she said, "Tomorrow, Ar-mand. But—" She blushed. When she was a child, reading "Ivanhoe" and "The Deerslayer," she used to practice blushing before the mirror. She never could do it. Yet she did it now. "But earlier," she finished.

Her astonishment factor clicked again, this time with the thought, why haven't I ever tried this before?

"Tomorrow night? You'll come?" he said. "You really will?"

"What time, Ar-mand?" she asked submissively.

"Well now. Hmp. Ah—say eleven?"

"Oh, it would be crowded here then. Ten, before the shows are over."

"I knew you were clever," he said admiringly.

She grasped the point firmly and pressed it. "There are always too many people," she said, looking around. "You know, we shouldn't leave together. Just in case."

He shook his head in wonder, and beamed.

"I'll just—" she paused, looking at his eyes, his mouth. "I'll just go, like that." She snapped her fingers. "No goodbyes . . ."

She skipped to her feet and ran out, clutching her purse. And as she passed the end of the bandstand, the guitarist, speaking in a voice just loud enough to reach her, and barely moving his lips, said,

"Lady, you ought to have your mouth washed out with bourbon."

HIS HONOR, THE SURROGATE ARMAND
Bluett, left his chambers early the next afternoon.
Dressed in a dark brown business suit and seeing alternately from the corners of his eyes, he taxied across
town, paid off the driver, and skulked down a narrow
street. He strolled past a certain doorway twice to be
sure he was not followed, and then dodged inside,
key in hand.

Upstairs, he went through the compact two-and-kitchenette with a fine-toothed comb. He opened all the windows and aired the place out. Stuffed between the cushions on the couch he found a rainbow-hued silk scarf redolent with cheap, dying scent. He dropped it in the incinerator with a snort. "Won't need *that* any more."

He checked the refrigerator, the kitchen shelves, the bathroom cabinet. He ran the water and tested the gas and the lights. He tried the end-table lamps, the torchère, the radio. He ran a small vacuum cleaner over the rugs and the heavy drapes. Finally, grunting with satisfaction, he went into the bathroom and shaved and showered. There followed clouds of talc and a haze of cologne. He pared his toenails, after which he stood before the cheval glass in various abnormal chest-out poses, admiring his reflection through a rose-colored ego.

He dressed carefully in a subdued hound's-tooth check and a tie designed strictly for the contracting pupil, returned to the mirror for a heady fifteen minutes, sat down and painted his nails with colorless polish, and wandered dreamily around fluttering his flabby hands and thinking detailed thoughts, reciting, half-aloud, little lines of witty, sophisticated dialogue. "Who polished your eyes?" he muttered, and "My dear, dear child, that was nothing, really nothing. A study in harmony, before the complex instrumentation of the flesh . . . no, she's not old enough for that one. Hm. You're the cream in my coffee. No! *I'm* not old enough for that."

So he passed the evening, very pleasantly indeed. At 8:30 he left, to dine sumptuously at a seafood restaurant. At 9:50 he was ensconced at the corner table at Club Nemo, buffing his glittering nails on his lapel and alternately wetting his lips and dabbing at them with a napkin.

At ten o'clock she arrived.

Last night he had risen to his feet as she crossed the dance floor. Tonight he was up out of his chair and at her side before she reached it.

This was Kay transformed. This was the concretion of his wildest dreams of her.

Her hair was turned back from her face in soft small billows which framed her face. Her eyes were skillfully shadowed, and seemed to have taken on a violet tinge with their blue. She wore a long cloak of some heavy material, and under it, a demure but skin-tight jacket of black ciré satin and a black hem-slashed skirt.

"Armand . . ." she whispered, holding out both hands.

He took them. His lips opened and closed twice before he could say anything at all, and then she was past him, walking with a long, easy stride to the table. Walking behind her, he saw her pause as the orchestra started up, and throw a glance of disdain at the guitarist. At the table she unclasped the cloak at her throat and let it fall away confidently. Armand Bluett was there to receive it as she slid into her chair. He stood there goggling at her for so long that she laughed at him. "Aren't you going to say anything at all?"

"I'm speechless," he said, and thought, my word, that came out effectively.

A waiter came, and he ordered for her. Daiquiri, this time. No woman he had ever seen reminded him less of a sherry flip.

"I am a very lucky man," he said. That was twice in a row he had said something unrehearsed.

"Not as lucky as I am," she said, and she seemed quite sincere as she said it. She put out just the tip of a pink tongue; her eyes sparkled, and she laughed. For Bluett, the room began to gyrate. He looked down at her hands, toying with the clasp of a tiny cosmetic case.

"I don't think I ever noticed your hands before," he said.

"Please do," she twinkled. "I love the things you say, Ar-mand," and she put her hands in his. They were long, strong hands with square palms and tapered fingers and what certainly must be the smoothest skin in the world.

The drinks came. He let go reluctantly and they both leaned back, looking at each other. She said, "Glad we waited?"

"Oh, yes. Hm. Yes indeed." Suddenly, waiting was intolerable. Almost inadvertently he snatched up his drink and drained it.

The guitarist fluffed a note. She looked pained. Armand said, "It's not too nice here tonight, is it?"

Her eyes glistened. "You know a better place?" she asked softly.

His heart rose up and thumped the lower side of his Adam's apple. "I certainly do," he said when he could.

She inclined her head with an extraordinary, controlled acquiescence that was almost like a deep pain to him. He threw a bill on the table, put her cloak over her shoulders, and led her out.

In the cab he lunged for her almost before the machine was away from the curb. She hardly seemed to move at all, but her body twisted away from him inside the cloak; he found himself with a double handful of cloth while Kay's profile smiled slightly, shaking its head. It was unspoken, but it was a flat "no." It was also a credit to the low frictional index of ciré satin.

"I never knew you were like this," he said.

"Like what?"

"You weren't this way last night," he floundered.

"What way, Ar-mand?" she teased.

"You weren't so—I mean, you didn't seem to be sure of yourself at all."

She looked at him. "I wasn't—ready."

"Oh, I see," he lied.

Conversation lapsed after that, until he paid off the cab at the street intersection near his hideout. He was beginning to feel that the situation was out of his control. If she controlled it, however, as she had so far, he was more than willing to go along.

Walking down the dirty, narrow street, he said, "Don't look at any of this, Kay. It's quite different upstairs."

"It's all the same, when I'm with you," she said, stepping over some garbage. He was very pleased.

They climbed the stairs, and he flung open the door with a wide gesture. "Enter, fair lady, the land of the lotus-eaters."

She pirouetted in and cooed over the drapes, the lamps, the pictures. He closed the door and shot the bolt, dropped his hat on the couch and stalked toward her. He was about to put his arms around her from behind when she darted away. "What a way to begin!" she sang. "Putting your hat there. Don't you know it's bad luck to put a hat on a bed?"

"This is my lucky day," he pronounced.

"Mine too," she said. "So let's not spoil it. Let's pretend we've been here forever, and we'll be here forever."

He smiled. "I like that."

"I'm glad. That way," she said, stepping away from a corner as he approached, "there's no hurry. Could we have a drink?"

"You may have the moon," he chanted. He opened the kitchenette. "What would you like?"

"Oh, how wonderful. Let me, let me. You go into the other room and sit down, Mister Man. This is woman's work." She shunted him out, and began to mix, busily.

Armand lounged back on the couch with his feet on the rock-maple coffee table, and listened to the pleasant clinking and swizzling noises from the other room. He wondered idly if he could get her to bring his slippers every evening.

She glided in, balancing two tall highballs on a small tray. She kept one hand behind her back as she knelt and put the tray down on the coffee table and slipped into an easy-chair.

"What are you hiding?" he asked.

"It's a secret."

"Come over here."

"Let's talk a little while first. Please."

"A little while." He sniggered. "It's your fault, Kay. You're so beautiful. Hm. You make me feel mad—impetuous." He began rubbing his hands together. She closed her eyes. "Armand . . ."

"Yes, my little one," he answered, patronizingly.

"Did you ever hurt anyone?"

He sat up. "I? Kay, are you afraid?" He puffed his chest out a bit. "Afraid of me? Why, I won't hurt you, baby."

"I'm not talking about me," she said, a little impatiently. "I just asked you—did you ever hurt anyone?"

"Why, of course not. Not intentionally, that is. You must remember—my business is justice."

"Justice." She said it as if it tasted good. "There are two ways of hurting people, Armand—outside, where it shows, and inside, in the mind, where it scars and festers."

"I don't follow you," he said, his pomposity returning as his confusion grew. "Whom have I ever hurt?"

"Kay Hallowell, for one," she said detachedly, "with the kind of pressure you've been putting on. Not because she's a minor; you are only a criminal on paper for that, and even that wouldn't apply in some states."

"Now, look here, young lady—"

"—but because," she went on calmly, "you have been systematically wrecking what faith she has in humanity. If there is a basic justice, then for that you are a criminal by its standards."

"Kay—what's come over you? What are you talking

about? I won't have any more of this!" He leaned back and folded his arms. She sat quietly.

"I know," he said, half to himself, "you're joking. Is that it, baby?"

In the same level, detached tone, she went on speaking. "You are guilty of hurting others in both the ways I mentioned. Physically, where it shows, and psychically. You will be punished in both those ways, *Justice* Bluett."

He blew air from his nostrils. "That is quite enough. I did not bring you here for anything like this. Perhaps I shall have to remind you, after all, that I am not a man to be trifled with. Hm. The matter of your estate—"

"I am not trifling, Armand." She leaned across the low table to him. He put up his hands. "What do you want?" he breathed, before he could stop himself.

"Your handkerchief."

"My h—*what?*"

She plucked it out of his breast pocket. "Thank you." As she spoke she shook it out, brought up two corners and knotted them together. She slipped her left hand through the loop and settled the handkerchief high on her forearm. "I am going to punish you first in the way it doesn't show," she said informatively, "by reminding you, in a way you can't forget, of how you once hurt someone else."

"What kind of nonsense—"

She reached behind her with her right hand and brought out what she had been hiding—a new, sharp, heavy cleaver.

Armand Bluett cowered away, back into the couch

cushions. "Kay—no! No!" he panted. His face turned green. "I haven't touched you, Kay! I only wanted to talk. I wanted to help you and—and your brother. Put that thing down, Kay!" He was drooling with terror. "Can't we be friends, Kay?" he whimpered.

"Stop it!" she hissed. She lifted the cleaver high, resting her left hand on the table and leaning toward him. Her face made, line upon plane upon carven curve, a mask of utter contempt. "I told you that your physical punishment comes later. Think about this while you wait for it."

The cleaver arced over and came down, with every ounce of a lithe body behind it. Armand Bluett screamed—a ridiculous, hoarse, thin sound. He closed his eyes. The cleaver crashed into the heavy top of the coffee-table. Armand twisted and scrabbled back into the cushions, crabbed sidewise and backward along the wall until he could go no farther. He stopped ludicrously, on all fours, on the couch, backed into the corner, sweat and spittle running off his chin. He opened his eyes.

It had apparently taken him only a split second to make the hysterical move, for she still stood over the table; she still held the handle of the cleaver. Its edge had buried itself in the thick wood, after passing through the flesh and bone of her hand.

She snatched up the bronze letter-opener and thrust it under the handkerchief on her forearm. As she straightened, bright arterial blood spouted from the stumps of three severed fingers. Her face was pale under the cosmetics, but not one whit changed otherwise; it still wore its proud, unadulterated contempt. She stood straight and tall, twisting the hand-kerchief with the handle of the letter-opener, making a tourniquet, and she stared him down. As his eyes fell, she spat, "Isn't this better than what you planned? Now you've got a part of me to keep for your very own. That's much better than using something and giving it back."

The spurting blood had slowed to a dribble as she twisted. Now she went to the chair on which she had left her cosmetic case. Out of it she worried a rubber glove. Holding the tourniquet against her side, she pulled the glove over her hand and snugged it around the wrist.

Armand Bluett began to vomit.

She shouldered into her cloak and went to the door.

When she had drawn back the bolt and opened it, she called back in a seductive voice, "It's been so wonderful, Ar-mand darling. Let's do it again soon . . ."

It took Armand's mind nearly an hour to claw its way up out of the pit of panic into which it had fallen. During the hour he hunkered there on the couch in his own filth, staring at the cleaver and the three still white fingers.

Three fingers.

Three *left* fingers.

Somewhere, deep in his mind, that meant something to him. At the moment he refused to let it surface. He feared it would. He knew it would. He knew that when it did, he would know consuming terror.

BOBBY DEAR, SHE WROTE, I CAN'T BEAR to think of you getting letters back with "address unknown" on them. I'm all right. That's first and foremost. I'm all right, monkey-face, and you're not to worry. Your big sister is *all right*.

I'm also all mixed up. Maybe in that nice orderly hospital this will make more sense to you. I'll try to make it short and simple.

I was working one morning at the office when that

awful Judge Bluett came in. He had to wait for a few minutes before he could see old Wattles Hartford, and he used it to make his usual wet soggy string of verbal passes. My brush worked fine until the seamy old weasel got on the subject of Daddy's money. You know that we'll get it when I'm 21—unless that old partnership deal comes up again. It would have to go to court. Bluett not only was the partner—he's the Surrogate. Even if we could get him disqualified from hearing the case, you know how he could fix anyone else who might take the bench. Well, the idea was that if I would be nice and sweet to Hizzoner, in any nasty way he wanted, the will wouldn't be contested. I was terribly frightened, Bobby; you know the rest of your training has to come out of that money. I didn't know what to do. I needed time to think. I promised to meet him that night, real late, in a night-club.

Bobby, it was awful. I was just at the point of blowing up, there at the table, when the old drooler left the room for a minute. I didn't know whether to fight or run away. I was scared, believe me. All of a sudden there was somebody standing there talking to me. I think he must be my guardian angel. Seems he had overheard the Judge talking to me. He wanted me to cut and run. I was afraid of him, too, at first, and then I saw his face. Oh, Bobby, it was such a *nice* face! He wanted to give me some money, and before I could say no he told me I could return it whenever I wanted to. He told me to get out of town right now—take a train, any train; he didn't even want to know which one. And before I could stop him he shoved $300 into my bag and walked off. The last thing he said was to accept a date for the next evening with the Judge. I couldn't do a thing—he'd only been there two minutes and he was talking practically every second of it. And then the Judge came back. I flapped my eyelids at the old fool like a lost woman, and cut out. I got a train to Eltonville twenty minutes later and didn't even register in a hotel when I got here. I waited around until the stores opened and bought an overnight case and a tooth brush and got myself a room. I slept a few hours and the very same afternoon I had a job in the only record shop in the place. It's $26 a week but I can make it fine.

Meanwhile I don't know what's happening back home. I'm sort of holding my breath until I hear something. I'm going to wait, though. We have time, and in the meantime, I'm all right. I'm not going to give you my address, honey, though I'll write often. Judge Bluett just might be able to get his hands on mail, some way. I think it pays to be careful. He's dangerous.

So, honey, that's the situation as far as it's gone. What next? I'll watch the home town papers for any item about His Dishonor the Surrogate, and hope for the best. As for you, don't worry your little square head about me, darling. I'm doing fine. I'm only making a few dollars a week less than I was at home and I'm a lot safer here. And the work isn't hard; some of the nicest people like music. I'm sorry I can't give you my exact address, but I do think it's better not to just now. We can let this thing ride for a year if we have

to, and small loss. Work hard, baby; I'm behind you a
thousand percent. I'll write often.

XXX                                    Your loving
                                       Big Sis Kay.


(This is the letter that Armand Bluett's hired sec-
ond-story man found in Undergraduate Robert Hallowell's room at the State Medical School.)

"YES—I AM PIERRE MONETRE. COME in." He stood aside and the girl entered.

"This is good of you, Mr. Monetre. I know you must be terribly busy. And probably you won't be able to help me at all."

"I might not if I were able," he said. "Sit down."

She took a molded plywood chair which stood at the end of the half desk, half lab bench which took up almost an end wall of the trailer. He looked at her coldly. Soft yellow hair, eyes sometimes slate-blue, sometimes a shade darker than sky-blue; a studied coolness through which he, with his schooled percep-tions, could readily see. She is disturbed, he thought; frightened and ashamed of it. He waited.

She said, "There's something I've got to find out. It happened years ago. I'd almost forgotten about it, and then saw your posters, and I remembered . . . I could be wrong, but if only—" She kneaded her hands together. Monetre watched them, and then returned his cold stare to her face.

"I'm sorry, Mr. Monetre. I can't seem to get to the point. It's all so vague and so—terribly important. The thing is, when I was a little girl, seven or eight years old, there was a boy in my class in school who ran away. He was about my age, and had some sort of horrible run-in with his stepfather. I think he was hurt. His hand. I don't know how badly. I was prob-ably the last one in town to see him. No one ever saw him again."

Monetre picked up some papers, shifted them, put them down again. "I really don't know what I can do about that, Miss—"

"Hallowell. Kay Hallowell. Please hear me out, Mr. Monetre. I've come thirty miles just to see you, be-cause I can't afford to pass up the slightest chance—"

"If you cry, you'll have to get out," he rasped. His voice was so rough that she started. Then he said, with gentleness, "Please go on."

"Th-thank you. I'll be quick . . . it was just after dark, a rainy, misty night. We lived by the highway, and I went out back for something . . . I forget . . .

anyway, he was there, by the traffic light. I spoke to him. He asked me not to tell anyone that I had seen him, and I never have, till now. Then—" she closed her eyes, obviously trying to bring back every detail of the memory— "—I think someone called me. I turned to the gate and left him. But I peeped out again, and saw him climbing on the back of a truck that was stopped for the light. It was one of your trucks. I'm sure it was. The way it was painted . . . and yesterday, when I saw your posters, I thought of it."

Monetre waited, his deep-set eyes expressionless. He seemed to realize, suddenly, that she had finished. "That happened twelve years ago? And, I suppose, you want to know if that boy reached the carnival."

"Yes."

"He did not. If he had, I should certainly have known of it."

"Oh . . ." It was a faint sound, stricken, yet resigned; apparently she had not expected anything else. She pulled herself together visibly, and said, "He was small for his age. He had very dark hair and eyes and a pointed face. His name was Horty—Horton."

"Horty . . ." Monetre searched his memory. There was a familiar ring to those two syllables, somehow. Now, where . . . He shook his head. "I don't remember any boy called Horty."

"Please try. *Please!* You see—" She looked at him searchingly, her eyes asking a question. He answered it, saying, "You can trust me."

She smiled. "Thank you. Well, there's a man, a horrible person. He was once responsible for that boy.

He's doing a terrible thing to me; it's something to do with an old law case, and he might be able to keep me from getting some money that is due me when I come of age. I need it. Not for myself; it's for my brother. He's going to be a doctor, and—"

"I don't like doctors," said Monetre. If there is a great bell for hatred as there is one for freedom, it rang in his voice as he said that. He stood up. "I know nothing about any boy named Horty, who disappeared twelve years ago. I am not interested in finding him in any case, particularly if doing so would help a man make a parasite of himself and fools of his patients. I am not a kidnapper, and will have nothing to do with a search which reeks of that and blackmail to boot. Good-by."

She had risen with him. Her eyes were round. "I—I'm sorry. Really, I—"

"Good-by." It was the velvet this time, used with care, used to show her that his gentleness was a virtuosity, an overlay. She turned to the door, opened it. She stopped and looked back over her shoulder. "May I leave you my address, just in case, some day, you—"

"You may not," he said. He turned his back on her and sat down. He heard the door close.

He closed his eyes, and his arched, slit nostrils expanded until they were round holes. Humans, humans, and their complex, useless, unimportant machinations. There was no mystery about humans; no puzzle. Everything human could be brought to light by asking simply, "What does it gain you?" . . . What could humans know of a life-form to which the idea of gain was alien? What could a human say of his crystal-kin, the living jewels which could communicate with each other and did not dare to, which could co-operate with each other and scorned to?

And what—he let himself smile—what would humans do when they had to fight the alien? When they were up against an enemy which would make an advance and then scorn to consolidate it—and then make a different *kind* of advance, in a different way, in another place?

He sank into an esoteric reverie, marshaling his crystallines against teeming, stupid mankind; losing, in his thoughts, the pointless perturbations of a girl in a search for a child long missing, for some petty gainful reason of her own.

"Hey—Maneater."

"*Damn* it! What now?"

The door opened diffidently. "Maneater, there's—"

"Come in, Havana, and speak up. I don't like mumblers."

Havana edged in, after setting his cigar down on the step. "There's a man outside wants to see you."

Monetre glowered over his shoulder. "Your hair's getting gray. What's left of it. Dye it."

"Okay, okay. Right away, this afternoon. I'm sorry." He shifted his feet miserably. "About this man—"

"I've had my quota for today," said Monetre. "Useless people wanting impossible things of no importance. Did you see that girl go out of here?"

"Yes. That's what I'm trying to tell you. So did this guy. See, he was waiting to see you. He asked Johnward where he could find you, and—"

"I think I'll fire Johnward. He's an advance man,

not an usher. What business has he, bringing people to annoy me?"

"I guess he thought you ought to see this one. A big-shot," said Havana timidly. "So when he got your trailer, he asked me were you busy. I told him yes, you were talking to someone. He said he'd wait. About then the door opens, and that girl comes out. She puts a hand on the side and turns back to say something to you, and this guy, this big-shot, he blows a fuse. No kidding, Maneater, I never seen anything like it. He grabs my shoulder. I'll have a bruise there for a week. He says, 'It's her! It's her!' and I says 'Who?' and he says, 'She mustn't see me! She's a devil! She cut those fingers off, and they've grown back again!'"

Monetre sat bolt upright and turned in his swivel chair to face the midget. "Go on, Havana," he said in his gentle voice.

"Well, that's all. 'Cept he ducked back behind Gogol's bally-platform and hunkered down out of sight, and peeped out at that girl as she walked past him. She never saw him."

"Where is he now?"

Havana glanced through the door. "Still right there. Looks pretty bad. I think he's having some kind of a fit."

Monetre left his chair and shot through the door, leaving it completely up to Havana whether he got out of the way or not. The midget leaped to the side, out of Monetre's direct path, but not far enough to avoid the bony edge of Monetre's pelvis, which glanced stunningly off Havana's pudgy cheekbone.

Monetre bounded to the side of the man who cowered down behind the bally platform. He knelt and
placed a sure hand on the man's forehead, which was
clammy and cold.

"It's all right now, sir," he said in a deep, soothing
voice. "You'll be perfectly safe with me." He urged
the idea "safe," because, whatever the cause might
be, the man was sodden, trembling, all but ecstatic
with fear. Monetre asked no questions, but kept
crooning, "You're in good hands now, sir. Quite safe.
Nothing can happen now. Come along; we'll have a
drink. You'll be all right."

The man's watery eyes fixed themselves on him,
slowly. Awareness crept into them, and a certain embarrassment. He said, "Hm. Uh—slight attack of—hm
. . . vertigo, you know. Sorry to be . . . hm."

Monetre courteously helped him up, picked up a
brown homburg and dusted it off. "My office is just
there. Do come in and sit down."

Monetre kept a firm hand on the man's elbow, led
him to the trailer, handed him up the two steps,
reached past him and opened the door. "Would you
like to lie down for a few minutes?"

"No, no. Thank you; you're very kind."

"Sit here, then. I think you'll find it comfortable.
I'll get you something that will make you feel better."
He fingered a simple combination latch, chose a bottle of tawny port. From a desk drawer he took a small
phial and put two drops of liquid into a glass, filling
it with the wine. "Drink this. It will make you feel
better. A little sodium amytal—just enough to quiet
your nerves."

"Thank you, thank—" He drank it greedily. "—you. Are you Mr. Monetre?"

"At your service."

"I am Judge Bluett. Surrogate, you know. Hm."

"I am honored."

"Not at all, not at all. I am the one who . . . I drove fifty miles to see you, sir, and would gladly have done twice that. You have a wide reputation."

"I hadn't realized it," said Monetre, and thought, this deflated creature is as insincere as I am. "What can I do for you?"

"Hm. Well, now. Matter of—ah—scientific interest. I read about you in a magazine, you know. Said you know more about fr—ah, strange people, and things like that, than anyone alive."

"I wouldn't say that," said Monetre. "I have worked with them for a great many years, of course. What was it you wanted to know?"

"Oh . . . the kind of thing you can't get out of reference books. Or ask any so-called scientist, for that matter; they just laugh at things that aren't in some book, somewhere."

"I have experienced that, Judge. I do not laugh readily."

"Splendid. Then I shall ask you. Namely, do you know anything about—ah—regeneration?"

Monetre cloaked his eyes. Would the fool ever get to the point? "What kind of regeneration? The girdle of the nematodes? Cellular healing? Or are you talking about old-time radio receivers?"

"Please," said the judge, and made a flabby gesture. "I'm quite the layman, Mr. Monetre. You'll have to use simple language. What I want to know is—how much of a restoration is possible after a serious cut?"

"How serious a cut?"

"Hm. Call it an amputation."

"Well, now. That depends, Judge. A fingertip, possibly. A chipped bone can grow surprisingly. You—you know of a case where a regeneration has been, shall we say, a bit more than normal?"

There was a long pause. Monetre noticed that the Judge was paling. He poured him more port, and filled a glass for himself. Excitement mounted within him.

"I do know of such a case. At least, I mean . . . hm. Well, it seemed so to me. That is, I saw the amputation."

"An arm? A leg, perhaps, or a foot?"

"Three fingers. Three whole fingers," said the Judge. "It would seem that they grew back. And in forty-eight hours. A well-known osteologist treated the whole thing as a great joke when I asked him about it. Refused to believe I was serious." Suddenly he leaned forward so abruptly that the loose skin of his jaw quivered. "Who was the girl who just left here?"

"An autograph hound," said Monetre in a bored tone. "A person of no importance. Do proceed."

The Judge swallowed with difficulty. "Her name is —Kay Hallowell."

"Perhaps so, perhaps so. Have you changed the subject?" asked Monetre impatiently.

"I have not, sir," the Judge answered hotly. "That girl, that monster—in good light, and right before my eyes, *chopped off three fingers of her left hand!*" He nodded, pushing his lower lip out, and sat back.

If he expected a sharp reaction, he was not disappointed. Monetre leaped to his feet and bellowed, "Havana!" He strode to the door and yelled again. "Where is that little fat—oh; there you are, Havana. Go and find that girl who just left here. Understand? Find her and bring her back. I don't care what you tell her; find her and bring her back here." He clapped his hands explosively. *"Run!"*

He returned to his chair, his face working. He looked at his hands, then at the judge. "You're quite sure of this."

"I am."

"Which hand?"

"The left." The Judge ran a finger around his collar. "Ah—Mr. Monetre. If that boy should bring her back here, why, ah—I, that is—"

"I gather you are afraid of her."

"Now, ah—I wouldn't say that," said the Judge. "Startled, yes. Hm. Wouldn't you be?"

"No," said Monetre. "You are lying, sir."

"I? Lying?" Bluett puffed up his chest and glowered at the carny boss.

Monetre half-closed his eyes and began ticking off items on his fingers. "It would seem that what frightened you a few minutes ago was the sight of that girl's left hand. You told the midget that the fingers had grown back. It was obviously the first time you had seen the hand regenerated. And yet you tell me that you have already consulted an osteologist about it."

"There are no lies involved," said Bluett stiffly. "True, I did see the restored hand when she stood in this doorway, and it was the first time. But I also saw her cut those fingers off!"

"Then why," asked Monetre, "come to me to ask questions about regeneration?" Watching the Judge flounder about for an answer, he added, "Come now, Judge Bluett. Either you have not stated your original purpose in coming here, or—you have seen a case of this regeneration before. Ah. I see that's it." His eyes began to burn. "I think you'd better tell me the whole story."

"That *isn't* it!" the Judge protested. "Really, sir, I am not enjoying this cross-questioning. I fail to see—"

Shrewdly, Monetre reached out to touch the fear which hovered so close to this wet-eyed man. "You are in greater danger than you suspect," he interrupted. "I know what that danger is, and I am probably the only man in the world who can help you. You will co-operate with me, sir, or you will leave this instant—and take the consequences." He said this with his flexible voice toned down to a soft, resonating diapason, which apparently frightened the Judge half out of his wits. The chain of imaginary horrors which mirrored themselves on Bluett's paling face must have been colorful, to say the least. Smiling slightly, Monetre leaned back in his chair and waited.

"M-may I . . ." The Judge poured himself more wine. "Ah. Now, sir. I must tell you at the outset that this whole matter has been one of—ah—conjecture on my part. That is, up until I saw the girl just now. By the way—I do not want to have her see me. Could you—"

"When Havana brings her back, I'll get you out of sight. Go on."

"Good. Thank you, sir. Well, some years ago I brought a child into my house. Ugly little monster. When he was seven or eight years old, he ran away from home. I have not heard of him since. I imagine he would be nineteen or so by this time—if he's alive. And—and there seems to be some connection between him and this girl."

"What connection?" Monetre prompted.

"Well, sh-she seemed to know something about him." As Monetre shifted his feet impatiently, he blurted, "Fact is, there was a little trouble. The boy was downright rebellious. I thrashed him and shoved him into a closet. His hand—quite accidentally, you realize—his hand was crushed in the hinge of the door. Hm. Yes—very unpleasant."

"Go on."

"I've been—ah—looking, you know—that is, if that boy has grown up, he might be resentful, you understand . . . besides, he was a most unbalanced child, and one never knows how these things might affect a weak mind—"

"You mean you feel guilty as hell and scared to boot, and you've been watching for a young man with some fingers missing. Fingers—get to the point! What has this to do with the girl?" Monetre's voice was a whip.

"I can't—say exactly," mumbled the Judge. "She seemed to know something about the boy. I mean, she hinted something about him—said that she was going to remind me of a way I had—hurt someone once. And then she took a cleaver and cut off her fingers. She disappeared. I had a man locate her. He found out she was due here—my man sent for me. That's all."

Monetre closed his eyes and thought hard. "There was nothing wrong with her fingers when she was in here."

"Damn it, I know that! But I tell you, I saw, with my own eyes—"

"All right, all right. She cut them off. Now, exactly why did you come here?"

"I—that's all. When something like that happens it makes you forget everything you know and start right from scratch. What I saw was impossible, and I began thinking in a way that let anything be possible . . . anyth—"

"Come to the point!" roared the Maneater.

"There is none!" Bluett roared back. They glared at each other for a crackling moment. "That's what I'm trying to tell you; I don't know. I remembered that child and his crushed fingers, and there was this girl and what she did. I began wondering if she and the boy were the same . . . I told you 'impossible' didn't matter any more. Well, the girl had a perfectly good hand before she chopped into it. If, somehow, she was that boy, he must have grown the fingers back. If he could do it once, he could do it again. If he knew he could do it again, he wouldn't be afraid to cut them off." The judge threw up his hands and shrugged, and let his arms fall limply. "So I began to wonder what manner of creature could grow fingers at will. That's all."

Monetre made wide eaves of his lids, his burning dark eyes studying the Judge. "This—boy who might be a girl," he murmured. "What was his name?"

"Horton. Horty, we called him. Vicious little scut."

"Think, now. Was there anything strange about him as a child?"

"I should say so! I don't think he was sane. Clinging to baby-toys—that sort of thing. And he had filthy habits."

"What filthy habits?"

"He was expelled from school for eating insects."

"Ah! Ants?"

"How did you know?"

Monetre rose, paced to the door and back. Excitement began to thump in his chest. "What baby-toys did he cling to?"

"Oh, I don't remember. It isn't important."

"I'll decide that," snapped Monetre. "Think, man! If you value your life—"

"I can't think! I can't!" Bluett looked up at the Maneater, and quailed before those blazing eyes. "It was some sort of a jack-in-the-box. A hideous thing."

"What did it look like? Speak up, damn it!"

"What does it—oh, all right. It was this big, and it had a head on it like a Punch—you know, Punch and Judy. Big nose and chin. The boy hardly ever looked at it. But he had to have it near him. I threw it away one time and the doctor made me find it and bring it back. Horton almost died."

"He did, eh?" grunted Monetre tautly, triumph-antly. "Now tell me—that toy had been with him since he was born, hadn't it? And there was something about it—some sort of jewelled button, or something glittery?"

"How did you know—" Bluett began again, and again quailed under the radiation of furious, excited impatience from the carny boss. "Yes. The eyes."

Monetre flung himself on the Judge. He grasped his shoulders, shook him. "You said 'eye,' didn't you? There was only one jewel?" he panted.

"Don't—don't—" wheezed Bluett, pushing weakly at Monetre's taloned hands. "I said 'eyes.' Two eyes. They were both the same. Nasty looking things. Seemed to have a light of their own."

Monetre straightened slowly, backed off. "Two of them," he breathed. "*Two . . .*"

He closed his eyes, his brain humming. Disappearing boy, fingers . . . fingers crushed. Girl . . . the right age, too . . . Horton. Horton . . . Horty. His mind looped and wheeled back over the years. A small brown face, peaked with pain, saying, "My folks called me Hortense, but everyone calls me Kiddo." Kiddo, who had arrived with a crushed hand, and had left the carnival two years ago. What had happened when she left? He had wanted something, wanted to examine her hand, and she left during the night.

That hand. When she first arrived, he had cleaned it up, trimmed away the ruined flesh, sewed it up. He had treated it every day for weeks, until the scar-

tissue was fused over, and there was no further danger of infection; and then, somehow or other he had
never looked at it again. Why not? Oh—Zena. Zena
had always told him how Kiddo's hand was getting
along.

He opened his eyes—slits, now. "I'll find him," he
snarled.

There was a knock at the door, and a voice. "Maneater—"

"It's the midget," babbled Bluett, leaping up.
"With the girl. What shall I—where shall—"

Monetre sent him a look which wilted him, tumbled him back in his chair. The carny boss rose and
stilted to the door, opening it a crack. "Get her?"

"Gosh, Maneater, I—"

"I don't want to hear it," said Monetre in a terrible
whisper. "You didn't bring her back. I sent you to get
her and you didn't do it." He closed the door with
great care and turned to the Judge. "Go away."

"Eh? Hm. But what about the—"

"Go away!" It was a scream. As his glare had made
Bluett limp, his voice stiffened him. The Judge was
on his feet and moving doorward before the scream
had ceased to be a sound. He tried to speak, and suc-
ceeded only in moving his wet mouth.

"I'm the only one in the world who can help you,"
said Monetre; and the Judge's face showed that this
easy, quiet, conversational tone was the most shocking thing of all. He went to the door and paused.
Monetre said, "I will do what I can, Judge. You'll
hear from me very soon, you may be sure of that."

"Ah," said the Judge. "Mm. Any thing I can do, Mr. Monetre. Call on me. Anything at all."

"Thank you. I shall certainly need your help." Monetre's bony features froze the instant he stopped speaking. Bluett fled.

Pierre Monetre stood staring at the space where the Judge's bloated face had just been. Suddenly he balled his fist and smashed it into his palm. "Zena!" said only his lips. He went pale with fury, weak with it, and went to his desk. He sat down, put his elbows on the blotter and his chin in his hand, and began to send out waves of feral hatred and demand.

*Zena!*
*Zena!*
*Here! Come Here!*

HORTY LAUGHED. HE LOOKED AT HIS left hand, at the three stubs of fingers which rose, like unspread mushrooms, from his knuckles, touched the scar-tissue around them with his other hand, and he laughed.

He rose from the studio couch and crossed the wide room to the cheval glass, to stare at his face, to stand back and look critically at his shoulders, his profile. He grunted in satisfaction and went to the telephone in the bedroom.

"Three four four," he said. His voice was resonant, well suited to the cast of his solid chin and his wide mouth. "Nick? This is Sam Horton. Oh, fine. Sure, I'll be able to play again. The doc says I was lucky. A broken wrist usually heals pretty stiff, but this one won't. No—don't worry. Hm? About six weeks. Positively . . . Gold? Thanks Nick, but I'll get along. No, don't worry—I'll yell if I need any. Thanks, though. Yeah, I'll drop by every once in a while. I was in there a couple days ago. Where did you find that three-chord bubblehead you have on guitar? He does by accident what Spike Jones does on purpose. No, I didn't want to hit him. I wanted to husk him." He laughed. "I'm kidding. He's okay. Well, thanks, Nick. 'Bye."

Going to the studio couch, he flung himself down with the confident relaxation of a well-fed feline. He pressed his shoulders luxuriously into the foam mattress, rolled and reached for one of the four books on the end table.

They were the only books in the apartment. Long ago he had learned of the physical encroachment of books, and the difficulties of overflowing book-cases. His solution was to get rid of them all, and make an arrangement with his dealer to send him four books a day—new books, on a rental basis. He read them all, and always returned them on the next day. It was a satisfactory solution, for him. He had total recall. What use, then, were book-cases?

He owned two pictures—a Markell, meticulously unmatched irregular shapes, varying in their apparent transparency, superimposed one on the other so that the tone of each affected the others, and so that the color of the background affected everything. The other was a Mondrian, precise and balanced, and conveying an almost-impression of something which could never quite be anything.

He owned, however, miles of magnetic tape on which was recorded a magnificent collection of music. Horty's fabulous mind could retain the whole mood of a book, and recall any part of it. It could do the same with music; but to recall music is to generate it to a certain degree, and there is a decided difference in the coloration of a mind which hears music and one which makes it. Horty could do both, and his music library made it possible for him to do either.

He had the classics and the romantics which had been Zena's favorites, the symphonies, concerti, ballads and virtuosic showpieces which had been his introduction to music. But his tastes had widened and deepened, and now included Honnegger and Copland, Shostakovitch and Walton. In the popular field he had discovered Tatum's somber chordings and the incredible Thelonius Monk. He had the occasionally inspired trumpet of Dizzy Gillespie, the bewildering cadenzas of Ella Fitzgerald, the faultless production of Pearl Bailey's voice. His criterion in all of it was humanity and the extensions of humanity. He lived with books that led to books, art that led him to conjecture, music that led him to worlds beyond worlds of experience.

Yet for all these riches, Horty's rooms were simply furnished. The only unconventional article of furniture was the tape recorder and reproducer—a massive incorporation of high-fidelity components which Horty had been led to assemble because of an ear that demanded every nuance, every overtone, of every instrumental voice. Otherwise his rooms were like anyone's comfortably appointed, tastefully decorated apartment. It occurred to him, fleetingly and at long intervals, that with his resources he could surround himself with automatic luxury-machines like back-kneading chairs and air-conditioned drying chambers for after his shower. But he was never moved in such directions. His mind was simply and steadily acquisitive. His analytical abilities were phenomenal, but he was seldom moved to use them extensively. Therefore to acquire knowledge was sufficient; its use could wait for demand, and there was little demand coexistent with his utter and demonstrable confidence in his own powers.

Halfway through his book he stopped, a puzzled expression in his eyes. It was as if a special sound had reached him—yet none had.

He closed the book and racked it, rose to stand listening, turning his head slightly as if he were trying to fix the source of the sensation.

The doorbell rang.

Horty stopped moving. It was not a freeze, the startled immobilization of a frightened animal. It was more a controlled, relaxed split second for thought. Then he moved again, balanced and easily.

At the door he paused, staring at the lower panel. His face tightened, and a swift frown rippled on his brow. He flung the door open.

She stood crookedly in the hallway, looking up at

him with her eyes. Her head was turned sidewise and a little downward. She had to strain her eyes painfully to meet his; she was only four feet tall.

She said, faintly, "Horty?"

He made a hoarse sound and knelt, pulling her into his arms, holding her with power and gentleness. "Zee . . . Zee, what happened? Your face, your—" He picked her up and kicked the door shut and carried her over to the studio couch, to sit with her across his knees, cradled in his arms, her head resting in the warm strong hollow of his right hand. She smiled at him. Only one side of her mouth moved. Then she began to cry, and Horty's own tears curtained from him the sight of her ravaged face.

Her sobs stopped soon, as if she were simply too tired to continue. She looked at his face, all of it, part by part. She brought her hand up and touched his hair. "Horty . . ." she whispered. "I loved you so much the way you were . . ."

"I haven't changed," he said. "I'm a big grown-up man now. I have an apartment and a job. I have this voice and these shoulders and I weigh a hundred pounds more than I did three years ago." He bent and kissed her quickly. "But I haven't changed, Zee. I haven't changed." He touched her face, a careful, feathery contact. "Do you hurt?"

"Some." She closed her eyes and wet her lips. Her tongue seemed unable to reach one corner of her mouth. "I've changed."

"You've *been* changed," he said, his voice shaking. "The Maneater?"

"Of course. You knew, didn't you?"

"Not really. I thought once you were calling me. Or he was . . . it was far away. But anyway, no one else would have—would . . . what happened? Do you want to tell me?"

"Oh yes. He—found out about you. I don't understand how. Your—that Armand Bluett—he's a judge or something now. He came to see the Maneater. He thought you were a girl. A big girl, I mean."

"I was, for a while." He smiled tensely.

"Oh. Oh, I see. Were you really at the carnival that day?"

"At the carnival? No. What day, Zee? You mean when he found out?"

"Yes. Four—no; five days ago. You weren't there. I don't under—" She shrugged. "Anyway, a girl came to see the Maneater and the Judge followed her and thought she was you. The Maneater thought so too. He sent Havana looking for her. Havana couldn't find her."

"And then the Maneater got hold of you."

"Mm. I didn't mean to tell him, Horty. I didn't. Not for a long time, anyway. I—forget." She closed her eyes again. Horty trembled suddenly, and then could breathe.

"I don't . . . remember," she said with difficulty.

"Don't try. Don't talk any more," he murmured.

"I want to. I've got to. He mustn't find you!" she said. "He's hunting for you right this minute!"

Horty's eyes narrowed and he said, "Good."

Her eyes were still closed. She said, "It was a long time. He talked very quietly. He gave me cushions and some wine that tasted like autumn. He talked about the carnival and Solum and Gogol. He mentioned 'Kiddo' and then talked about the new flat cars and the commissary tent and the trouble with the roustabouts' union. He said something about the musicians' union and something about music and something about the guitar and then about the act we used to have. Then he was off again about the menageries and the shills and the advance men, and back again. You see? Just barely mentioning you and going away and coming back and back. All night, Horty, all, all *night!*"

"Sh-h-h."

"He wouldn't ask me! He talked with his head turned away watching me out of the corners of his eyes. I sat and tried to sip the wine, and tried to eat when Cooky brought dinner and midnight lunch and breakfast, and tried to smile when he stopped for a minute. He didn't touch me, he didn't hit me, he didn't *ask* me!"

"He did later," breathed Horty.

"Much later. I don't remember . . . his face over me like a moon, once. I hurt all over. He shouted. Who is Horty, where is Horty, who is Kiddo, why did I hide Kiddo. . . . I woke up and woke up. I don't remember the times I slept, or fainted, or whatever it was. I woke up with my blood in my eyes, drying, and he was talking about the ride mechanics and the power for the floodlights. I woke up in his arms, he was whispering in my ear about Bunny and Havana, they must have known what Horty was. I woke up on the floor. My knee hurt. There was a terrible light. I jumped up with the pain of it. I ran out the door and fell down, my knee wouldn't work, it was in the afternoon and he caught me and dragged me back again and threw me on the floor and made the light again. He had a burning glass and he gave me vinegar to drink. My tongue swelled, I—"

"Sh-h-h. Zena, honey, hush. Don't say any more."

The flat, uninflected voice went on. "I lay still when Bunny looked in and the Maneater didn't know she saw what he was doing and Bunny ran away and Havana came and hit the Maneater with a piece of pipe and the Maneater broke his neck he's going to die and I—"

Horty's eyelids felt dry. He raised a careful hand and slapped her smartly across her undamaged cheek. "Zena. *Stop it!*"

At the impact she uttered a great shriek, and screamed, "I don't *know* any more, *truly* I don't!" and burst into painful, writhing sobs. Horty tried to speak to her but could not be heard through her weeping. He stood, turned, put her down gently on the couch, ran and wrung out a cloth in cold water and bathed her face and wrists. She stopped crying abruptly and fell asleep.

Horty watched her until her breathing assured him that she was at peace. He put his head slowly down beside hers as he knelt on the floor beside the couch. Her hair was on his forehead. Half-crossing his arms, he grasped his elbows and began to pull them. He kept the tension until his shoulders and chest throbbed with pain. He needed to be near her, would not move, yet must relieve the black tension of fury which built in him, and the work his muscles did against each other saved his sanity without the slight-est movement to disturb the sleeping girl. He knelt there for a long time.

At breakfast the next morning she could laugh again. Horty had not moved her or touched her ex-cept to remove her shoes and cover her with a down quilt. In the small hours of the morning he had taken a pillow from the bedroom and put it on the floor between the studio couch and the door, and had stretched out to listen to her breathing and, with feline attention, to each sound from the stairway and hall outside.

He was standing, bent over her, when she opened her eyes. He said immediately, "I'm Horty and you're safe, Zee." The spiralling panic in her eyes died un-born, and she smiled.

While she bathed, he took her clothes to a neigh-borhood machine laundry and in half an hour was back with them washed and dried. The food he had picked up on the way was not needed; she had break-fast well on the way when he returned—"gas-house" eggs (fried in the center of slices of bread punched out with a water glass) and crisp bacon. She took the groceries from him and scolded him. "Kippers—pa-paya juice—Danish ring. Horty, that's *company* eat-ments!"

He smiled, more at her courage and her resilience than at her protests. He leaned against the wall with his arms folded, watching her hobbling about the kitchen, draped from neck to heels in what was, for him, a snug-fitting bathrobe, and tried not to think of the fact that she had used it at all. He understood, though, seeing the limp, seeing what had happened to her face . . .

It was a gay breakfast, during which they happily played "Remember when—" which is, in the final analysis, the most entrancing game in the world. Then there was a silent time, when to each, the sight of the other was enough communication. At last Horty asked, "How did you get away?"

Her face darkened. The effort for control was evident—and successful. Horty said, "You'll have to tell me everything, Zee. You'll have to tell me about—me, too."

"You've found out a lot about yourself." It was not a question.

Horty waved this aside. "How did you get away?"

The mobile side of her face twitched. She looked down at her hands, slowly lifted one, put it on and around the other, and as she talked, squeezed. "I was in a coma for days, I guess. Yesterday I woke up on my bunk, in the trailer. I knew I had told him everything—except that I knew where you were. He still thinks you are that girl.

"I heard his voice. He was at the other end of the trailer, in Bunny's room. Bunny was there. She was crying. I heard the Maneater taking her away. I waited and then dragged myself outside and over to Bunny's door. I got in. Havana was there on the bed with a stiff thing around his neck. It hurt him to talk. He said the Maneater was taking care of him, fixing his neck. He said the Maneater is going to make Bunny do a job for him." She looked up swiftly at

Horty. "He can, you know. He's a hypnotist. He can make Bunny do anything."

"I know." He considered her. "Why the hell didn't he use it on you?" he flared.

She fingered her face. "He can't. He—it doesn't work like that on me. He can reach me, but he can't make me do anything. I'm too—"

"Too what?"

"Human," she said.

He stroked her arm and smiled at her. "That you are . . . Go on."

"I went back to my part of the trailer and got some money and a few other things and left. I don't know what the Maneater will do when he learns I'm gone. I was very careful, Horty. I hitch-hiked fifty miles and then took a bus to Eltonville—that's three hundred miles from here—and a train from there. But I know he'll find me somehow, sooner or later. He doesn't give up."

"You're safe here," he said, and there was blued steel in his soft voice.

"It isn't me! Oh, Horty—don't you understand? It's you he's after!"

"What does he want with me? I left the carnival three years ago and it didn't seem to bother him much." He caught her eye; she was looking at him in amazement. "What is it?"

"Aren't you curious about yourself at all, Horty?"

"About myself? Well, sure. Everybody is, I guess. But about what, especially?"

She was silent a moment, thinking. Abruptly she

asked, "What have you done since you left the carnival?"

"I've told you in my letters."

"The bare outlines, yes. You got a furnished room and lived there for a while, reading a lot and feeling your way. Then you decided to grow. How long did that take?"

"About eight months. I got this by mail and moved in at night so no one saw me, and changed. Well, I had to. I'd be able to get a job as a grown man. I buskined a while—you know, playing the clubs for whatever the customers would throw to me—and bought a really good guitar and went to work at the Happy Hours. When that closed I went to Club Nemo. Been there ever since, biding my time. You told me I'd know when it was time . . . that's always been true."

"It would be," she nodded. "Time to stop being a midget, time to go to work, time to start on Armand Bluett—you'd know."

"Well, sure," he said, as if the fact deserved no further comment. "And when I needed money, I wrote things . . . some songs and arrangements, articles and even a story or two. The stories weren't so good. It's easy to put things together, but awful hard to make them up. Hey—you don't know what I did to Armand, do you?"

"No." She looked at his hand. "It has something to do with that, hasn't it?"

"It has." He inspected it and smiled. "Last time you saw my hand like this was about a year after I came to the carnival. Want to know something? I lost these fingers just three weeks ago."

"And they've grown that much?"

"It doesn't take as long as it did," he said.

"It did start slowly," she said.

He looked at her, seemed about to ask a question, and then went on. "One night at Club Nemo he walked in with her. I'd never dreamed that I'd seen them together—I know what you're thinking! I always thought of them at the same time! Ah, but that was check and balance. Good and evil. Well . . ." He drank coffee. "They sat right where I could hear them talk. He was the oily wolf and she was the distressed maiden. It was pretty disgusting. So, he got up to powder his nose, and I made like Lochinvar. I mixed right in. I gave her some succinct language and some carfare, and she got away, after promising him a date for the next night."

"You mean she got away from him for the moment."

"Oh no. She got clear away, by train. I don't know where she went. Well, I sat there chording that guitar and thinking hard. You said that I'd always know when it was time. I knew that night that it was time to get Armand Bluett. Time to start, that is. He gave me a treatment once that lasted for six years. The least I could do was to give him a long stretch too. So I made my plans. I put in a tough night and day." He stopped, smiling without humor.

"Horty—"

"I'll tell it, Zee. It's simple enough. He got his date. Took the gal to a sybaritic little pest-hole he had hidden away in the slums. He was very easy to lead along the primrose paving. At the critical point his 'conquest' said a few well-chosen words about cruelty to children and left him to mull them over while staring at the three fingers she had chopped off as souvenirs."

Zena glanced at his left hand again. "Uh! What a treatment! But Horty—you got ready in one night and day?"

"You don't know the things I can do," he said. He rolled back his sleeve. "Look."

She stared at the brown, slightly hairy right fore-arm. Horty's face showed deep concentration. There was no tension; his eyes were quiet and his brow unfurrowed.

For a moment the arm remained unchanged. Suddenly the hair on it moved—*writhed*. One hair fell off; another; a little shower of them, finding their way down among the small checks of the tablecloth. The arm remained steady and, like his brow, showed no tension beyond its complete immobility. It was naked now, and the creamy brown color that was typical of both him and Zena. But—was it? Was it the effect of staring with such concentration? No; it was actually paler, paler and more slender as well. The flesh on the back of the hand and between the fingers contracted until the hand was slim and tapered rather than square and thick as it had been.

"That's enough," said Horty conversationally, and smiled. "I can restore it in the same length of time. Except for the hair, of course. That will take two or three days."

"I knew about this," she breathed. "I did know, but I don't think I ever really believed . . . your control is quite complete?"

"Quite. Oh, there are things I can't do. You can't create or destroy matter. I could shrink to your size, I suppose. But I'd weigh the same as I do now, pretty much. And I couldn't become a twelve-foot giant overnight; there's no way to assimilate enough mass quickly enough. But that job with Armand Bluett was simple. Hard work, but simple. I compacted my shoulders and arms and the lower part of my face. Do you know I had twenty-eight toothaches the whole time? I whitened my skin. The hair was a wig, of course, and as for the female form deevine, that was taken care of by what Elliot Springs calls the 'bust-bucket and torso-twister trade.'"

"How can you joke about it?"

His voice went flat as he said, "What should I do; grind my teeth *every* minute? This kind of wine needs a shot of bubbles every now and then, honey, or you can't swallow much. No; what I did to Armand Bluett was just a starter. I'm making him do it himself. I didn't tell him who I am. Kay's out of the picture; he doesn't know who she is or who I am or, for that matter, who he is himself." He laughed; an unpleasant sound. "All I gave him was a powerful association with three ruined fingers from 'way back. They'll work in his sleep. The next thing I do to him will be as good—and nothing like that at all."

"You'll have to change your plans some."

"Why?"

"Kay isn't out of the picture. I'm beginning to understand now. She came out to the carnival to see the Maneater."

"*Kay* did? But why?"

"I don't know. Anyway, the Judge followed her there. She left, but Bluett and the Maneater got together. I know one thing, though. Havana told me— the Judge is terrified of Kay Hallowell."

Horty slapped the table. "With her hand intact! Oh, how wonderful! Can you imagine what that must have been?"

"Horty, darling—it isn't all fun. Don't you see that that's what started all this—that's what made the Maneater suspect that 'Kiddo' was something else besides a girl midget? Don't you realize that the Maneater thinks you and Kay are the same one, no matter what the Judge thinks?"

"Oh, my God."

"You remember everything you hear," said Zena. "But you just don't figure things out very fast, sweetheart."

"But—but—getting smashed up like this . . . Zena, it's my fault! It's as if I'd done it to you!"

She came around the table and put her arms around him, pulling his head to her breast. "No, darling. That was coming to me, from years back. If you want to blame someone—besides the Maneater— blame me. It was my fault for taking you in twelve years ago."

"What did you do it for? I never really knew."

"To keep you away from the Maneater."

"Away fr—but you kept me right next to him!"

"The last place in the world he'd think of looking."

"You're saying he was looking for me then."

"He's been looking for you ever since you were one year old. And he'll find you. He'll find you, Horty."

"I hope he does," grated Horty. The doorbell rang.

There was a frozen silence. It rang again.

"I'll go," said Zena, rising.

"You will like hell," said Horty roughly. "Sit down."

"It's the Maneater," she whimpered. She sat down.

Horty stood where he could look through the living room at the front door. Studying it, he said, "It isn't. It's—it's—well, what do you know! Old Home Week!"

He strode out and flung the door open. "Bunny!"

"Wh-Excuse m—is this where . . ." Bunny hadn't changed much. She was a shade more roly-poly, and perhaps a little more timid.

"Oh, Bunny . . ." Zena came running unevenly out, tripped on the hem of the bathrobe. Horty caught her before she could fall. The girls hugged each other frantically, shouting tearful endearments over the rich sound of Horty's relieved laughter. "But darling, how did you find—" "It's so good to—" "I thought you were—" "You doll! I never thought I'd—"

"*Cut!*" roared Horty. "Bunny, come in and have some breakfast."

Startled, she looked at him, her albino eyes round. Gently he asked, "How's Havana?"

Without taking her eyes off his face, Bunny fumbled for Zena and held on. "Does he know Havana?"

"Honey," said Zena, "That's *Horty!*"

Bunny shot Zena a rabbit-like glance, craned to

peer behind Horty, and suddenly seemed to realize just what Zena had said. "That?" she demanded, pointing. "Him?" She stared. "He's—Kiddo, too?"

Horty grinned. "That's right."

"He grew," said Bunny inanely. Zena and Horty bellowed with laughter, and, as Horty had done once so long ago, so Bunny gaped from one to the other, sensed that they were laughing with and not at her, and joined her tinkling giggle to the noise. Still laughing, Horty went into the kitchen and called out, "You still take canned milk and half a teaspoon of sugar, Bunny?" and Bunny began to cry. Into Zena's shoulder she sobbed happily. "It is Kiddo, it is, it is . . ."

Horty put the steaming cup on the end table and settled down beside the girls. "Bunny, how in time did you find me?"

"I didn't find you. I found Zee. Zee, maybe Havana's goin' to die."

"I—remember," Zee whispered. "Are you sure?"

"The Maneater did what he could. He even called in another doctor."

"He *did*? Since when has he taken to doctors?"

Bunny sipped her coffee. "You just can't know how he's changed, Zee. I couldn't believe it myself until he did that, called a doctor in, I mean. You know about m-me and Havana. You know how I feel about what the Maneater did to him. But—it's as if he had come up from under a cloud that he's lived with for years. He's really changed. Zee, he wants you to come back. He's *so* sorry about what happened. He's really broken up."

"Not enough," muttered Horty.

"Does he want Horty to come back too?"

"Horty—oh. Kiddo." Bunny looked at him. "He couldn't do an act now. I don't know, Zee. He didn't say."

Horty noticed the swift, puzzled frown on Zena's brow. She took Bunny's upper arm and seemed to squeeze it impatiently. "Honey—start from the beginning. Did the Maneater send you?"

"Oh no. Well, not exactly. He's changed so, Zee. You don't believe me . . . Well, you'll see for yourself. He needs you and I came to get you back, all by myself."

"Why?"

"Because of Havana!" Bunny cried. "The Maneater might be able to save him, don't you see? But not when he's all torn apart by what he did to you."

Zena turned a troubled face to Horty. He rose. "I'll fix you a bite to eat, Bunny," he said. A slight side-wise movement of his head beckoned to Zena; she acknowledged it with an eyelid and turned back to Bunny. "But how did you know where I was, honey?"

The albino leaned forward and touched Zena's cheek. "You poor darling. Does it hurt much?"

Horty, in the kitchen, called, "Zee! What did you do with the tabasco?"

"Be right back, Bun," said Zee. She hobbled across to the kitchen. "It should be right there on the . . . yes. Oh—you haven't started the toast! I'll do it, Horty."

They stood side by side at the stove, busily. Under his breath Horty said, "I don't like it, Zee."

She nodded. "There's something . . . we've asked her twice, three times, how she found this place, and she hasn't said." She added clearly, "See? *That's* the way to make toast. Only you have to watch it."

A moment later, "Horty. How did you know who it was at the door?"

"I didn't. Not really. I knew who it *wasn't*. I know hundreds of people, and I knew it wasn't any of them." He shrugged. "That left Bunny. You see?"

"I can't do that. Nobody I know can do that. 'Cept maybe the Maneater." She went to the sink and clattered briskly. "Can't you tell what people are thinking?" she whispered when she came close to him again.

"Sometimes, a little. I never tried, much."

"Try now," she said, nodding toward the living room.

His face took on that unruffled, deeply occupied expression. At the same moment there was a flash of movement past the open kitchen door. Horty, who had his back to it, turned and sprang through into the living room. "Bunny!"

Bunny's pink lips curled back from her teeth like an animal's and she scuttled to the front door, whipped it open and was gone. Zena screamed. "My purse! She's got my purse!"

In two huge bounds Horty was in the hall. He pounced on Bunny at the head of the stairs. She squealed and sank her teeth into his hand. Horty clamped her head under his arm, jamming her chin against his chest. Having taken a bite, she was forced to keep it—and meanwhile was efficiently gagged.

Inside, he kicked the door closed and pitched Bunny to the couch like a sack of sawdust. Her jaws did not relax; he had to lean over her and pry them apart. She lay with her eyes red and glittering, and blood on her mouth.

"Now, what do you suppose made her go off like that?" he asked, almost casually.

Zena knelt by Bunny and touched her forehead. "Bunny. Bunny, are you all right?"

No answer. She seemed conscious. She kept her mad ruby eyes fixed on Horty. Her breath came in regular, powerful pulses like those of a slow freight. Her mouth was rigidly agape. "I didn't do anything to her," said Horty. "Just picked her up."

Zena rescued her handbag from the floor and fumbled through it. Seemingly satisfied, she set it down on the coffee table. "Horty, what did you do in the kitchen just now?"

"I—sort of . . ." He frowned. "I thought of her face, and I made it kind of open like a door, or—well, blow away like fog, so I could see inside. I didn't see anything."

"Nothing at all?"

"She moved," he said simply.

Zena began to knead her hands together. "Try again."

Horty went to the couch. Bunny's eyes followed him. Horty folded his arms. His face relaxed. Bunny's eyes closed immediately. Her jaw slackened. Zena barked, "Horty—be careful!"

Without moving otherwise, Horty nodded briefly. For a moment nothing happened. Then Bunny trembled. She threw out an arm, clenched her small hand. Tears appeared between her lids, and she relaxed. In a few seconds she began to move vaguely, purposelessly, as if unfamiliar hands tested her motor centers. Twice she opened her eyes; once she half sat up, and then lay back. At last she released a long, shuddering sigh, pitched almost as low as Zena's voice, and lay still, breathing deeply.

"She's asleep," said Horty. "She fought me, but now she's asleep." He fell into a chair and covered his face for a moment. Zena watched him restore himself as he had restored his whitened arm earlier. He sat up briskly and said, his voice strong again, "It was more than her strength, Zee. She was full to the brim with something that wasn't hers."

"Is it all gone now?"

"Sure. Wake her and see."

"You've never done anything like this before, Horty? You seem as sure of yourself as old Iwazian." Iwazian was the carnival's photo-gallery operator. He had only to take a picture to know how good it was; he never looked at a proof.

"You keep saying things like that," said Horty with a trace of impatience. "There are things a man can do and things he can't. When he does something, what's the point of wondering whether or not he's actually done it? Don't you think he knows?"

"I'm sorry, Horty. I keep underestimating you." She sat beside the albino midget. "Bunny," she cooed. "Bunny . . ."

Bunny turned her head, turned it back, opened her eyes. They seemed vague, unfocussed. She turned them on Zena, and recognition crept into them. She looked around the room, cried out in fear. Zena held her close. "It's all right, darling," she said. "That's Kiddo, and I'm here, and you're all right now."

"But how—where—"

"Sh-h. Tell us what's happened. You remember the carnival? Havana?"

"Havana's goin' to die."

"We'll try to help, Bunny. Do you remember coming here?"

"Here." She looked around, as if one part of her mind were trying to catch up with the rest. "The Maneater told me to. He was nothing but eyes. After a while I couldn't even see his eyes. His voice was inside my head. I don't remember," she said piteously. "Havana's going to die." She said this as if it were the first time.

"We'd better not ask her questions now," said Zena.

"Wrong," said Horty. "We'd better, and fast." He bent over Bunny. "How did you find this place?"

"I don't remember."

"After the Maneater talked inside your head, what did you do?"

"I was on a train." Her answers were almost vague; she did not seem to be withholding information—rather, she seemed unable to extend it. It had to be lifted out.

"Where did you go when you got off the train?"

"A bar. Uh—Club . . . Nemo. I asked the man where I could find the fellow who hurt his hand."

Zena and Horty exchanged a look. "The Maneater said Zena would be with this fellow."

"Did he say the man was Kiddo? Or Horty?"

"No. He didn't say. I'm hungry."

"All right, Bunny. We'll get you a big breakfast in a minute. What were you supposed to do when you found Zena? Bring her back?"

"No. The jewels. She had the jewels. There had to be two of them. He'd give me twice what he gave Zena if I came back without them. But he'd kill me if I came with only one."

"How he's changed," Zena said, scornful horror in her voice.

"How did he know where I was?" Horty demanded.

"I don't know. Oh; that girl."

"What girl?"

"She's a blonde girl. She wrote a letter to someone. Her brother. A man got the letter."

"What man?"

"Blue. Judge Blue."

"Bluett?"

"Yes, Judge Bluett. He got the letter and it said the girl was working in a record shop in town. There was only one record shop. They found her easily."

"*They found her?* Who?"

"The Maneater. And that Blue. Bluett."

Horty brought his fists together. "Where is she?"

"The Maneater's got her at the carnival. Can I have my breakfast now?"

HORTY LEFT.

He slipped into a light coat and found his wallet and keys, and he left. Zena screamed at him. Intensity injected raucousness into her velvet voice. She caught his arm; he did not shake her off, but simply kept moving, dragging her as if she were smoke in the suction of his movement. She turned to the table, snatched up her bag, found two glittering jewels. "Horty, wait, wait!" She held out the jewels. "Don't you remember, Horty? Junky's eyes, the jewels—they're *you*, Horty!"

He said, "If you need anything at all, no matter what, call Nick at Club Nemo. He's all right," and opened the door.

She hobbled after him, caught at his coat, missed her hold, staggered against the wall. "Wait, wait. I have to tell you, you're not ready, you just don't *know*!" She sobbed. "Horty, the Maneater—"

Halfway down the stairs he turned. "Take care of Bunny, Zee. Don't go out, not for anything. I'll be back soon."

And he left.

Holding the wall, Zena crept down the hall and into the apartment. Bunny sat on the couch, sobbing with fright. But she stopped when she saw Zena's twisted face, and ran to her. She helped her to the easy-chair and crouched on the floor at her feet, hugging her legs, her round chin against Zena's knees. The vibrant color was gone from Zena; she stared dryly down, black eyes in a grey face.

The jewels fell from her hand and glittered on the rug. Bunny picked them up. They were warm, probably from Zena's hand. But the little hand was so cold . . . They were hard, but Bunny felt that if she squeezed them they would be soft. She put them on Zena's lap. She said nothing. She knew, somehow, that this was not the time to say anything.

Zena said something. It was unintelligible; her voice was a hoarseness, nothing more. Bunny made a small interrogative sound, and Zena cleared her throat and said, "Fifteen years."

Bunny waited quietly after that, for minutes, wondering why Zena did not blink her eyes. Surely that
must hurt her . . . she reached up presently and
touched the lids. Zena blinked and stirred uneasily.
"Fifteen years I've been trying to stop this from happening. I knew what he was the instant I saw those
jewels. Maybe even before . . . but I was sure when
I saw the jewels." She closed her eyes; it seemed to
give more vitality to her voice, as if her intense gaze
had been draining her. "I was the only one who
knew. The Maneater only hoped. Even Horty didn't
know. Only me. Only me. Fifteen years—"

Bunny stroked her knee. A long time passed. She
became certain that Zena was asleep, and had begun
to think thoughts of her own when the deep, tired
voice came again.

"They're alive." Bunny looked up; Zena's hand was
over the jewels. "They think and they speak. They
mate. They're alive. These two are Horty."

She sat up and pushed her hair back. "That's how
I knew. We were in that diner, the night we found
Horty. A man was robbing our truck, remember? The
man put his knee on these crystals, and Horty got
sick. He was indoors and a long way from the truck
but he knew. Bunny, do you remember?"

"Mm-hm. Havana, he used to talk about it. Not to
you, though. We always knew when you didn't want
to talk, Zee."

"I do now," said Zena wearily. She wet her lips.
"How long have you been with the show, Bun?"

"I guess eighteen years."

"Twenty for me. Almost that, anyway. I was with

Kwell Brothers when the Maneater bought into it. He had a menagerie. He had Gogol and a pinhead and a two-headed snake and a bald squirrel. He used to do a mind-reading act. Kwell sold out for nothing. Two late springs and a tornado taught Kwell all the carny he ever wanted to know. Lean years. I stuck with the show because I was there, mostly. Just as tough there as anywhere else." She sighed, scanning over twenty years. "The Maneater was obsessed by what he called a hobby. Strange people aren't his hobby. Carny isn't his hobby. Those things are because of his hobby." She lifted the jewels and clicked them together like dice. "These are his hobby. These things sometimes make strange people. When he got a new freak—" (The word jolted both of them as she said it)—"he kept it by him. He got into show business so he could keep them and make money too. that's all. He kept them and studied them and made more of them."

"Is that really what makes strange people?"

"No! Not all of them. You know about glands and mutations, and all that. These crystals make them too, that's all. They do it—I *think* they do it—on purpose."

"I don't understand, Zee."

"Bless your heart! Neither do I. Neither does the Maneater, although he knows an awful lot about them. He can talk to them, sort of."

"How?"

"It's like his mind-reading. He puts his mind on them. He—hurts them with his mind until they do what he wants."

"What does he want them to do?"

"Lots of things. They all amount to one thing, though. He wants a—a middle-man. He wants them to make something that he can maybe talk to, give orders to. Then the middle-man would turn around and make the crystals do what he wanted."

"I guess I'm sort of stupid, Zee."

"No you're not, honey . . . oh. Bunny, Bunny, I'm so *glad* you're here!" She pulled the albino up into the chair and hugged her fervently. "Let me talk, Bun. I've got to talk! Years and years, and I haven't said a word . . ."

"I won't understand one word in ten, I bet."

"Yes you will, lamb. Comfy? Well . . . you see, these crystals are a sort of animal, kind of. They're not like any other animal that ever lived on earth. I don't think they came from anywhere on earth. The Maneater told me he sees a picture sometimes of white and yellow stars in a black sky, the way space would look away outside the earth. He thinks they drifted here."

"He told you? You mean he talked to you about them?"

"By the hour. I guess everybody has to talk to someone. He talked to me. He threatened to kill me, time and time again, if I ever said a word. But that's not why I kept it a secret. See, he was good to me, Bunny. He's mean and crazy, but he was always good to me."

"I know. We used to wonder."

"I didn't think it made any difference to anyone. Not at first, not for years. When I did learn what he was really trying to do, I *couldn't* tell anyone; no one would've believed me. All I could do was to learn as much as I could and hope I could stop him when the time came."

"Stop him from what, Zee?"

"Well—look; let me tell you a little more about the crystals. Then you'll see. These crystals used to *copy* things. I mean, one would be near a flower, and it would make another flower almost like it. Or a dog, or a bird. But mostly they didn't come out right. Like Gogol. Like the two-headed snake."

"Gogol is one of those?"

Zena nodded. "The Fish-Boy. I think he was supposed to be a human being. No arms, no legs, no teeth, and he can't sweat so he has to be kept in a tank or he'll die."

"But what do the crystals do that for?"

She shook her head. "That's one of the things the Maneater was trying to find out. There isn't anything regular about the things the crystals make, Bunny. I mean, one will look like the real thing and another will come up all strange, and another won't live at all, it's such a botch. That's why he wanted a middle-man—someone who could communicate with the crystals. He couldn't except in flashes. He could no more understand them than you or I could understand advanced chemistry or radar or something. But one thing did not come clear. There are different kinds of crystals; some are more complicated than others, and can do more. Maybe they're all the same kind, but some are older. They never helped each other; didn't seem to have anything to do with each other.

"But they bred. The Maneater didn't know that. He knew that sometimes a pair of crystals would sometimes stop responding when he hurt them. At first he thought they were dead. He dissected one pair. And once he gave a couple to old Worble."

"I remember him! He used to be a strong man, but he was too old. He used to help the cook, and all. He died."

"Died—that's one way to say it. Remember the things he used to whittle?"

"Oh, yes—dolls and toys and all like that."

"That's right. He made a jack-in-the-box and used these for eyes." She tossed the crystals and caught them. "He was always giving things away to kids. He was a good old man. I know what happened to that jack-in-the-box. The Maneater never found out, but Horty told me. Somehow or other it passed from hand to hand and got into an orphanage. That's where Horty was, when he was a tiny baby. Inside of six months they were a part of Horty—or he was a part of them."

"But what about Worble?"

"Oh, maybe a year later the Maneater began wondering if the crystals bred, and what happened when they did. He was afraid that he had given away two big, well-developed crystals that weren't dead after all. When Worble told him he had put them in toys he made and some kid had them, he didn't know where, why, the Maneater hit him. Knocked him down. Old Worble never woke up again though it was two weeks before he died. No one knew about it but me. It was out behind the cook-tent. I saw."

"I never knew," breathed Bunny, her ruby eyes wide.

"No one did," Zena repeated. "Let's have some coffee—why, *honey!* You never did get your breakfast, you poor baby!"

"Oh gosh," said Bunny, "that's all right. Go on talking."

"Come into the kitchen," she said as she rose stiffly. "No, don't be surprised when the Maneater seems to be inhuman. He—*isn't* human."

"What is he, then?"

"I'll get to it. About the crystals; the Maneater says that the closest you can come to the way they make things—plants and animals, and so on, is to say they *dream* them. You dream sometimes. You know how the things in your dreams are sometimes sharp and clear, and sometimes fuzzy or crooked or out of proportion?"

"Yup. Where's the eggs?"

"Here, dear. Well, the crystals dream sometimes. When they dream sharp and clear they make pretty good plants, and real rats and spiders and birds. They usually don't, though. The Maneater says they're erotic dreams."

"What d'ye mean?"

"They dream when they're ready to mate. But some are too—young, or undeveloped, and maybe some just don't find the right mate at that time. But when they dream that way, they change molecules in a plant and make it like another plant, or change a pile of mold into a bird . . . no one can say what they'll choose to make, or why."

"But—why should they make things so they can mate?"

"The Maneater doesn't think they do it so they *can* mate, exactly," said Zena, her voice patient. She skillfully flipped an egg in the pan. "He calls it a by-product. It's as if you were in love and you were thinking of nothing but the one you love, and you made a song. Maybe the song wouldn't be about your lover at all. Maybe it'd be about a brook, or a flower, or something. The wind. Maybe it wouldn't be a whole song, even. That song would be a by-product. See?"

"Oh. And the crystals make things—even complete things—like Tin Pan Alley makes songs."

"Something like it." Zena smiled. It was the first smile in a long while. "Sit down, honey; I'll bring the toast. Now—this is my guess—when two crystals mate, something different happens. They make a whole thing. But they don't make it from just anything the way the single crystals do. First they seem to die together. For weeks they lie like that. After that they begin a together-dream. They find something near them that's alive, and they make it over. They replace it, cell by cell. You can't see the change going on in the thing they're replacing. It might be a dog; the dog will keep on eating and running around; it will howl at the moon and chase cats. But one day —I don't know how long it takes—it will be completely replaced, every bit of it."

"Then what?"

"Then it can change itself—if it ever thinks of changing itself. It can be almost anything if it wants to be."

Bunny stopped chewing, thought, swallowed, and asked, "Change how?"

"Oh, it could get bigger or smaller. Grow more limbs. Go into a funny shape—thin and flat, or round like a ball. If it's hurt it can grow new limbs. And it could do things with thought that we can't even imagine. Bunny, did you ever read about werewolves?"

"Those nasty things that change from wolves to men and back again?"

Zena sipped coffee. "Mmm. Well, those are mostly legends, but they could have started when someone saw a change like that."

"You mean these crystal-things aren't new on earth?"

"Oh, heavens no! The Maneater says they're arriving and living and breeding and dying here all the time."

"Just to make strange people and werewolves," breathed Bunny in wonder.

"No, darling! Making those things is nothing to them! They live a life of their own. Even the Maneater doesn't know what they do, what they think about. The things they make are absent-minded things, like doodles on a piece of paper that you throw away. But the Maneater thinks he could understand them if he could get that middle-man."

"What's he want to understand a crazy thing like that for?"

Zena's small face darkened. "When I found that out, I began listening carefully—and hoping that some day I could stop him. Bunny, the Maneater hates people. He hates and despises all people."

"Oh, yes," said Bunny.

"Even now, with the poor control he has over the crystals, he's managed to make some of them do what he wants. Bunny, he's planted crystals in swampland with malaria mosquito eggs all around them. He's picked up poisonous coral snakes in Florida and planted them in Southern California. Things like that. It's one of the reasons he keeps the carnival. It covers the country, the same route year after year. He goes back and back, finding the crystals he's planted, seeing how much harm they've done to people. He keeps finding more. He finds them all over. He walks in the woods and out on the prairies, and every once in a while he sends out a—a kind of thought he knows how to do. It hurts the crystals. When they feel pain, he knows it. He hunts around, hurting the crystals until their pain leads him right to them. But anyway, there are plenty around. They look like pebbles or clods until they're cleaned."

"Oh, how—how awful!" Tears brightened Bunny's eyes. "He ought to be—killed!"

"I don't know if he can be killed."

"You mean he really is one of those things from the crystals?"

"Do you think a human being could do what he does?"

"But—what would he do if he got that middle-man?"

"He'd train him up. Those creatures that are made by two crystals, they're whatever they think they are. The Maneater would tell the middle-man that he was a servant; he was under orders. The middle-man would believe him, and think that of himself. Through him the Maneater would have real power over the crystals. He could probably even make them mate, and dream-together any horrible thing he wanted. He could spread disease and plant-blight and poison until there wouldn't be a human being left on earth! And the worst thing about it is that the crystals don't even seem to want that! They're satisfied to go on as they are, making a flower or a cat once in a while, and thinking their own thoughts, and living whatever strange sort of life they live. They aren't after people! They just don't *care*."

"Oh, Zee! And you've been carrying all this around with you for years!" Bunny ran around the table and kissed her. "Oh, baby, why didn't you tell someone?"

"I didn't dare, sweetheart. They would think I was out of my mind. And besides—there's Horty."

"What about Horty?"

"Horty was a baby in an orphanage when, somehow, that toy with the crystal eyes was brought in. The crystals picked on him. It all fits. He told me that when the jack-in-the-box—he called it Junky—was taken away from him; he almost died. The doctors there thought it was some kind of psychosis. It wasn't, of course; the child was in some strange bondage to the married crystals and could not exist away from them. It seems that it was far simpler to leave the toy with the child—it was an ugly toy, Horty tells me—than to try to cure the psychosis. In any case, Junky went along with Horty when he was adopted—by that Armand Bluett, incidentally; that judge."

"He's awful! He looks all soft and—*wet*."

"The Maneater has been looking for one of those twin-crystal creatures for twenty years or more, only he didn't know it. Why, the very first crystal he found was probably one of a pair, and he didn't realize it. Not ever—not until he found out about Horty. He guessed it, but he never *knew* until now. I knew that night we picked up Horty. The Maneater would give everything he owns in the world for Horty—a human. Not a human; Horty isn't human and hasn't been since he was a year old. But you know what I mean."

"And that would be his middle-man?"

"That's right. So when I saw what Horty was, I jumped at the chance to hide him in the last place in the world Pierre Monetre would think of looking—right under his nose."

"Oh, Zee! What a terrible chance to take! He was bound to find out!"

"It wasn't too much of a chance. The Maneater can't read my mind. He can prod it; he can call me in a strange way; but he can't find out what's in it. Not the way Horty did on you before. The Maneater hypnotized you to make you steal the jewels and bring them back. Horty went right into your mind and cleared all that away."

"I—I remember. It was crazy."

"I kept Horty by me and worked on him constantly. I read everything I could get my hands on and fed it to him. Everything, Bunny—comparative anatomy and history and music and mathematics and chemistry—everything I could think of that would help him to a knowledge of human things. There's an old Latin saying, Bunny: *Cogito ergo sum*—'I think, therefore I am.' Horty is the essence of that saying. When he was a midget he believed he was a midget. He didn't grow. He never thought of his voice changing. He never thought of applying what he learned to himself; he let me make all his decisions for him. He digested everything he learned in a reservoir with no outlet, and it never touched him until he decided himself that it was time to use it. He has eidetic memory, you know."

"What's that?"

"Camera memory. He remembers perfectly everything he has seen or read or heard. When his fingers began to grow back—they were smashed hopelessly, you know—I kept it a secret. That was the one thing that would have told the Maneater what Horty was. Humans can't regenerate fingers. Single-crystal creatures can't either. The Maneater used to spend hours in the dark, in the menagerie tent, trying to force the bald squirrel to grow hair, or trying to put gills on Gogol the Fish Boy, by prodding at them with his mind. If any of them had been twin-crystal creatures, they would have repaired themselves."

"I think I see. And what you were doing was to convince Horty that he was human?"

"That's right. He had to identify himself first and foremost with humanity. I taught him guitar for that reason, after his fingers grew back, so that he could learn music quickly and thoroughly. You can learn more music theory in a year on guitar than you can in three on a piano, and music is one of the most human of human things . . . He trusted me completely because I never let him think for himself."

"I—never heard you talk like this before, Zee. Like out of books."

"I've been playing a part too, sweet," said Zena gently. "First, I had to keep Horty hidden until he had learned everything I could teach him. Then I had to plan some way to make him stop the Maneater, without danger of the Maneater's making a servant of him."

"How could he do that?"

"I think the Maneater is a single-crystal thing. I think if Horty could only learn to use that mental whip that the Maneater has, he could destroy him with it. If I should kill the Maneater with a bullet, it won't kill his crystal. Maybe that crystal will mate, later, and produce him all over again—with all the power that a twin-crystal creature has."

"Zee, how do you know the Maneater isn't a twin-crystal thing?"

"I don't," Zee said bleakly. "If that's the case, then I can only pray that Horty's estimate of himself as a human being is strong enough to fight what the Maneater wants to make of him. Hating Armand Bluett is a human thing. Loving Kay Hallowell is another. Those are two things that I needled him with, drilled into him, teased him about, until they became part of his blood and bone."

Bunny was silent before this bitter flood of words. She knew that Zena loved Horty; that she was enough of a woman to feel Kay Hallowell's advent as a deep menace to her; that she had fought and won against the temptation to steer Horty away from Kay; and that, more than anything else, she was face to face with terror and remorse now that her long campaign had come to a head.

She watched Zena's proud, battered face, the lips which drooped slightly on one side, the painfully canted head, the shoulders squared under the voluminous robe, and she knew that here was a picture she would never forget. Humanity is a concept close to the abnormals, who are wistfully near it, who state their membership with aberrated breath, who never cease to stretch their stunted arms toward it. Bunny's mind struck a medallion of this torn and courageous figure—a token and a tribute.

Their eyes met, and slowly Zena smiled. "Hi, Bunny . . ."

Bunny opened her mouth and coughed, or sobbed. She put her arms around Zena and snuggled her chin into the cool hollow of the dark-skinned neck. She closed her eyes tight to squeeze away tears. When she opened them she could see again. And then she couldn't speak.

She saw, over Zena's shoulder through the kitchen door, out in the living room, a huge, gaunt figure. Its lower lip swung loosely as it bent over the coffee table. Its exquisite hands plucked up one, two jewels. It straightened, sent her a look of dull pity from its sage-green face, and went silently out.

"Bunny, darling, you're hurting me."

*Those jewels are Horty,* Bunny thought. *Now I'll tell her Solum has taken them back to the Maneater.* Her face and her voice were as dry and as white as chalk as she said, "You haven't been hurt yet . . ."

HORTY POUNDED UP THE STAIRS AND burst into his apartment. "I'm walking under water," he gasped. "Every damn thing I reached for is snatched away from me. Everything I do, everywhere I go, it's too early or too late or—" Then he saw Zena on the easy-chair, her eyes open and staring, and Bunny crouched at her feet. "What's the matter here?"

Bunny said, "Solum came in when we were in the

kitchen and took the jewels and we couldn't do anything and Zena hasn't said a word since and I'm scared and I don't know what to do—hoo . . ." and she began to cry.

"Oh Lord." He was across the room in two strides. He lifted Bunny up and hugged her briefly and set her down. He knelt beside Zena. "Zee—"

She did not move. Her eyes were all pupil, windows to a too-dark night. He tilted her chin up and fixed his gaze on her. She trembled and then cried out as if he had burned her, twisted into his arms. "Don't, don't . . ."

"Oh, I'm sorry, Zee. I didn't know it would hurt you."

She leaned back and looked up at him, seeing him at last. "Horty, you're all right . . ."

"Well, sure. What's this about Solum?"

"He got the crystals. Junky's eyes."

Bunny whispered, "For twelve years she's been keeping them away from the Maneater, Horty; and now—"

"You think the Maneater sent him for them?"

"Must have. I guess he must have followed me, and waited until he saw you leave. He was in here and out again before we could do so much as turn and look."

"Junky's eyes . . ." There was the time he had almost died, as a child, when Armand threw the toy away. And the time when the tramp had crushed them under his knee, and Horty, in the lunch room two hundred feet away, had felt it. Now the Maneater might . . . oh, no. This was too much.

Bunny suddenly clapped her hand to her mouth. "Horty—I just thought—the Maneater wouldn't've sent Solum by himself. He wanted those jewels . . . you know how he gets when he wants something. He can't bear to wait. He must be in town right now."

"No." Zena rose stiffly. "No, Bun. Unless I'm quite wrong, he was here and is on his way back to the carnival. If he thinks Kay Hallowell is Horty, he'll want to have the jewels where he can work on them and watch her at the same time. I'll bet he's burning up the road back to the carnival this minute."

Horty moaned. "If only I hadn't gone out! I might've been able to stop Solum, maybe even get to the Maneater and— Damn it! Nick's car was in the garage; first I had to find Nick and borrow it, and then I had to get a parked truck out from in front of the garage, and then there was no water in the radiator, and—oh, you know. Anyway, I have the car now. It's downstairs. I'm going to take off right now. In three hundred miles I ought to be able to catch up with . . . how long ago was Solum here?"

"An hour or so. You just can't, Horty. And what will happen to you when he goes to work on those jewels, I hate to think."

Horty took out keys, tossed and caught them. "Maybe," he said suddenly, "Just maybe we can—" He dove for the phone.

Listening to him talk rapidly into the instrument, Zena turned to Bunny. "A plane. But of course!"

Horty put the phone down, looking at his watch. "If I can get out to the airport in twelve minutes I can get a feeder flight."

"You mean 'we.' "

"You're not coming. This is my party, from here on out. You kids have been through enough."

Bunny was pulling on her light coat. "I'm going back to Havana," she said grimly, and for all her baby features, her face showed case-hardened purpose.

"You're not going to leave me here," said Zena flatly. She went for her coat. "Don't argue with me, Horty. I have a lot to tell you, and maybe a lot to do."

"But—"

"I think she's right," said Bunny. "She has a lot to tell you."

The plane was wobbling out to the runway when they arrived. Horty drove right out onto the tarmac, horn blasting, and it waited. And after they were settled in their seats, Zena talked steadily. They were ten minutes away from their destination when she was finished.

After a long, thoughtful pause, Horty said, "So that's what I am."

"It's a big thing to be," said Zena.

"Why didn't you tell me all this years ago?"

"Because there were too many things I didn't know. There still are . . . I didn't know how much the Maneater might be able to dig out of your mind if he tried; I didn't know how deep your convictions on yourself had to go before they settled. All I tried to do was to have you accept, without question, that you were a human being, a part of humanity, and grow up according to that idea."

He turned on her suddenly. "Why did I eat ants?"

She shrugged. "I don't know. Perhaps even two crystals can't do a perfect job. Anyway your formic acid balance was out of adjustment. (Did you know the French word for 'ant' is *fourmi*? They're full of the stuff.) Some kids eat plaster because they need calcium. Some like burned cake for the carbon. If you had an imbalance, you can bet it would be an important one."

The flaps went down; they felt the braking effect. "We're coming in. How far is the carnival from here?"

"About four miles. We can get a cab."

"Zee, I'm going to leave you outside the grounds somewhere. You've been through too much."

"I'm going in with you," said Bunny firmly. "But Zee— I think he's right. Please stay outside until—until it's over."

"What are you going to do?"

He spread his hands. "Whatever I can. Get Kay out of there. Stop Armand Bluett from whatever filthy thing he plans to do with her and her inheritance. And the Maneater . . . I don't know, Zee. I'll just have to play it as it comes. But *I* have to do it. You've done all you can. Let's face it; you're not fast on your feet just now. I'd have to keep looking out for you."

"He's right, Zee. Please—" said Bunny.

"Oh, be careful, Horty—*please* be careful!"


No bad dream can top this, Kay thought. Locked in a trailer with a frightened wolf and a dying midget, with a madman and a freak due back any minute. Wild talk about missing fingers, about living jewels, and about—wildest of all—Kay not being Kay, but someone or something else.

Havana moaned. She wrung out a cloth and sponged his head again. Again she saw his lips tremble and move, but words stuck in his throat, gurgled and fainted there. "He wants something," she said. "Oh, I wish I knew what he wanted! I wish I knew, and could get it quickly . . ."

Armand Bluett leaned against the wall by the window, one sack-suited elbow thrust through it. Kay knew he was uncomfortable there and that, probably, his feet hurt. But he wouldn't sit down. He wouldn't get away from the window. Oh no. He might want to yell for help. Old Crawly-Fingers was suddenly afraid of her. He still looked at her wet-eyed and drooling, but he was terrified. Well, let it go. No one likes having his identity denied, but in this case it was all right with her. Anything to keep a room's-breadth between her and Armand Bluett.

"I wish you'd leave that little monster alone," he snapped. "He's going to die anyway."

She turned a baleful glance on him and said nothing. The silence stretched, punctuated only by the Judge's painful foot-shifting. Finally he said, "When Mr. Monetre gets back with those crystals, we'll soon find out who you are. And don't tell me again that you don't know what all this is about," he snapped.

She sighed. "I don't know. I wish you'd stop shouting like that. You can't jolt information out of me that I haven't got. And besides, this little fellow's sick."

The Judge snorted, and moved even closer to the

window. She had an impulse to go over there and growl at him. He'd probably go right through the wall. But Havana moaned again. "What is it, fellow? What is it?"

Then she stiffened. Deep within her mind she sensed a presence, a concept connected somehow with delicate, sliding music, with a broad pleasant face and a good smile. It was as if a question had been asked of her, to which she answered silently, *I'm here. I'm all right—so far.*

She turned to look at the Judge, to see if he shared the strange experience. He seemed tense. He stood with his elbow on the sill, nervously buffing his nails on his lapel.

And a hand came through the window.

It was a mutilated hand. It rose into the trailer like the seeking head and neck of a waterfowl, passed in over Armand's shoulder and spread itself in front of has face. The thumb and index fingers were intact. The middle finger was clubbed; the other two were mere buttons of scar-tissue.

Armand Bluett's eyebrows were two stretched semi-circles, bristling over bulging eyes. The eyes were as round as the open mouth. His upper lip turned back and upward, almost covering his nostrils. He made a faint sound, a retch, a screech, and dropped.

The hand disappeared through the window. There were quick footsteps outside, around to the door. A knock. A voice. "Kay. Kay Hallowell. Open up."

Inanely, she quavered, "Wh-who is it?"

"Horty." The doorknob rattled. "Hurry. The Man-eater's due back, but quick."

"Horty. I—the door's locked."

"The key must be in the Judge's pocket. Hurry."

She went with reluctant speed to the prone figure. It lay on its back, the head propped against the wall, the eyes screwed shut in a violent psychic effort to shut out the world. In the left jacket pocket were keys on a ring—and one single. This she took. It worked.

Kay stood blinking at sunlight. "Horty."

"That's right." He came in, touched her arm, grinned. "You shouldn't write letters. Come on, Bunny."

Kay said, "They thought I knew where you were."

"You do." He turned away from her and studied the supine form of Armand Bluett. "What a sight. Something the matter with his stomach?"

Bunny had arrowed to the bunk, knelt beside it. "Havana . . . Oh Havana . . ."

Havana lay stiffly on his back. His eyes were glazed and his lips pouted and dry. Kay said, "Is—is he . . . I've done what I could. He wants something. I'm afraid he—" She went to the bedside.

Horty followed. Havana's pale chubby lips slowly relaxed, then pursed themselves. A faint sound escaped. Kay said, "I *wish* I knew what he wants!" Bunny said nothing. She put her hands on the hot cheeks, gently, but as if she would wrest something up out of him by brute force.

Horty frowned. "Maybe I can find out," he said. Kay saw his face relax, smoothed over by a deep placidity. He bent close to Havana. The silence was so profound, suddenly, that the carnival noises outside seemed to wash in on them, roaring.

The face Horty turned to Kay a moment later was twisted with grief. "I know what he wants. There may not be time before the Maneater gets here . . . but— There's got to be time," he said decisively. He turned to Kay. "I've got to go to the other end of the trailer. If he moves—" indicating the Judge— "hit him with your shoe. Preferably with a foot in it." He went out, his hand, oddly, on his throat, kneading.

"What's he going to do?"

Bunny, her eyes fixed on Havana's comatose face, answered, "I don't know. Something for Havana. Did you see his face when he went out? I don't think Havana's going to—to—"

From the partition came the sound of a guitar, the six open strings brushed lightly. The A was dropped, raised a fraction. The E was flatted a bit. Then a chord . . .

Somewhere a girl began to sing to the guitar. *Stardust.* The voice was full and clear, a lyric soprano, pure as a boy's voice. Perhaps it was a boy's voice. There was a trace of vibrato at the ends of the phrases. The voice sang to the lyric, just barely trailing the beat, not quite ad lib, not quite stylized, and as free as breathing. The guitar was not played in complicated chords, but mostly in swift and delicate runs in and about the melody.

Havana's eyes were still open, and still he did not move. But his eyes were wet now, and not glazed,

and gradually he smiled. Kay knelt beside Bunny.
Perhaps she knelt only to be nearer . . . Havana
whispered, through his smile, "Kiddo."

When the song was done, his face relaxed. Quite
clearly he said "Hey." There was a world of compli-
ment in the single syllable. After that, and before
Horty came back, he died.

Entering, Horty did not even glance at the cot. He
seemed to be having trouble with his throat. "Come
on," he said hoarsely. "We've got to get out of here."

They called Bunny and went to the door. But
Bunny stayed by the bunk, her hands on Havana's
cheeks, her soft round face set.

"Bunny, come on. If the Maneater comes back—"

There was a step outside, a thump against the wall
of the trailer. Kay wheeled and looked at the suddenly darkened window. Solum's great sad face filled
it. Just then Horty screamed shrilly and dropped
writhing to the floor. Kay turned to face the opening
door.

"Good of you to wait," said Pierre Monetre, looking about.

ZENA HUDDLED ON THE EDGE OF THE lumpy motel bed and whimpered. Horty and Bunny had been gone for nearly two hours; for the past hour, depression had grown over her until it was like bitter incense in the air, like clothes of lead sheeting on her battered limbs. Twice she had leapt up and paced impatiently, but her knee hurt her and drove her back to the bed, to punch the pillow impotently, to lie passive and watch the doubts circling endlessly about her. Should she have told Horty about himself? Should she not have given him more cruelty, more ruthlessness, about more things than revenging himself on Armand Bluett? How deep had her training gone in the malleable entity which was Horty? Could not Monetre, with his fierce, directive power undo her twelve years' work in an instant? She knew so little; she was, she felt, so small a thing to have undertaken the manufacture of a—a human being.

She wished, fiercely, that she could burrow her mind into the strange living crystals, as the Maneater tried to do, but completely, so that she could find the rules of the game, the facts about a form of life so alien that logic seemed not to work on it at all. The crystals had a rich vitality; they created, they bred, they felt pain; but to what end did they live? Crush one, and the others seemed not to mind. And why, why did they make these "dream-things" of theirs, laboriously, cell by cell—sometimes to create only a horror, a freak, an unfinished, unfunctional monstrosity, sometimes to copy a natural object so perfectly that there was no real distinction between the copy and its original; and sometimes, as in Horty's case, to create something new, something that was not a copy of anything but, perhaps, a mean, a living norm on the surface, and a completely fluid, polymorphic being at its core? What was their connection with these creations? How long did a crystal retain control of its product—and how, having built it, could it abruptly leave it to go its own way? And when the rare syzygy occurred by which two crystals made something like Horty—when would they release him to be his own creature . . . and what would become of him then?

Perhaps the Maneater had been right when he had described the creatures of the crystals as their dreams —solid figments of their alien imaginations, built any way they might occur, patterned on partial suggestions pictured by faulty memories of real objects. She knew—the Maneater had happily demonstrated—that there were thousands, perhaps millions of the crystals on earth, living their strange lives, as oblivious to humanity as humanity was to them, for the life-cycles, the purposes and aims of the two species were completely separate. Yet—how many men walked the earth who were not men at all; how many trees, how many rabbits, flowers, amoebae, sea-worms, redwoods, eels and eagles grew and flowered, swam and hunted and stood among their prototypes with none knowing that they were an alien dream, having, apart from the dream, no history?

"Books," Zena snorted. The books she had read! She had snatched everything she could get her hands on that would give her the slightest lead on the nature of the dreaming crystals. And for every drop of information she had gained (and passed on to Horty) about physiology, biology, comparative anatomy, philosophy, history, theosophy and psychology, she had taken in a gallon of smug certitude, of bland assumptions that humanity was the peak of creation. The answers . . . the books had answers for everything. A new variety of manglewort appears, and some learned pundit places his finger alongside his nose and pronounces, "Mutation!" Sometimes, certainly. But—always? What of the hidden crystal-creature dreaming in a ditch, absently performing, by some strange telekinesis, a miracle of creation?

She loved, she worshipped Charles Fort, who refused to believe that any answer was the only answer.

She looked at her watch yet again, and whimpered. If she only knew; if she could only guide him . . . if she could get guidance herself, somewhere, somewhere . . .

The doorknob turned. Zena froze, staring at it. Something heavy pressed against the door. There was no knock. The crack between door and frame, high up, widened. Then the bolt let go, and Solum burst into the room.

His loose-skinned, grey-green face and dangling lower lip seemed to pull more than usual at the small, inflamed eyes. He took a half-step back to swing the door closed behind him, and crossed the room to her, his great arms away from his body as if to check any move she might make.

His presence told her some terrible news. No one knew where she was but Horty and Bunny, who had left her in this tourist cabin before they crossed the highway to the carnival. And when last heard of, Solum had been on the road with the Maneater.

So—the Maneater was back, and he had contacted Bunny or Horty, or both, and, worst of all, he had been able to extract information that neither would give willingly.

She looked up at him out of a tearing flurry of deadening resignation and mounting terror. "Solum—"

His lips moved. His tongue passed over his brilliant pointed teeth. He reached for her, and she shrank back.

And then he dropped to his knees. Moving slowly, he took her tiny foot in one of his hands, bent over it with an air that was, unmistakably, reverence.

He kissed her instep, ever so gently, and he wept. He released her foot and crouched there, immersed in great noiseless shuddering sobs.

"But, *Solum*—" she said, stupidly. She put out a hand and touched his wet cheek. He pressed it closer. She watched him in utter astonishment. Long ago she used to wonder at what went on in the mind behind this hideous face, a mind locked in a silent, speechless universe, with all the world pouring in through the observant eyes and never an expression, never a conclusion or an emotion coming out.

"What is it, Solum?" she whispered. "Horty—"

He looked up and nodded rapidly. She stared at him. "Solum—can you hear?"

He seemed to hesitate; then he pointed to his ear, and shook his head. Immediately he pointed to his brow, and nodded.

"Oh-h-h . . ." Zena breathed. For years there had been idle arguments in the carnival as to whether the Alligator-skinned Man was really deaf. There was instance after instance to prove both that he was, and that he was not. The Maneater knew, but had never told her. He was—telepathic! She flushed as she thought of it, the times that carnies, half-kidding, had hurled insults at him; worse, the horrified reactions of the customers.

184

"But— What's happened? Have you seen Horty? Bunny?"

His head bobbed twice.

"Where are they? Are they safe?"

He thumbed toward the carnival, and shook his head gravely.

"Th-the Maneater's got them?"

Yes.

"And the girl?"

Yes.

She hopped off the bed, strode away and back, ignoring the pain. "He sent you here to get me?"

Yes.

"But why don't you scoop me up and take me back, then?"

No answer. He motioned feebly. She said, "Let's see. You took the jewels when he asked you to . . ."

Solum tapped his forehead, spread his hands. Suddenly she understood. "He hypnotized you then."

Solum shook his head slowly.

She understood that it had been a matter of indifference to him. But this time it was different. Something had happened to change his mind, and drastically.

"Oh, I wish you could talk!"

He made anxious, lateral circular motions with his right hand. "Oh, of *course!*" she exploded. She limped to the splintery bureau and her purse. She found her pen; she had no paper but her checkbook. "Here, Solum. Hurry. Tell me!"

His huge hands enveloped the pen, completely hid the narrow paper. He wrote rapidly while Zena wrung her hands in impatience. At last he handed it to her. His script was delicate, almost microscopic, and as neat as engraving.

He had written, tersely, "M. hates people. Me too. Not so much. M. wants help, I helped him. M. wanted Horty so he could hurt more people. I didn't care. Still helped. People never liked me.

"I am human, a little. Horty is not human at all. But when Havana was dying, he wanted Kiddo to sing. Horty read his mind. He knew. There was no time. There was danger. Horty knew. Horty didn't save himself. He made Kiddo's voice. He sang for Havana. Too late then. M. came. Caught him. Horty did this so Havana could die happy. It didn't help Horty. Horty knew; did it anyway. Horty is love. M. is hate. Horty more human than I am. I am ashamed. You made Horty. Now I help you."

Zena read it, her eyes growing very bright. "Havana's dead, then."

Solum made a significant gesture, twisting his head in his hands, pointing to his neck, snapping his fingers loudly. He shook his fist at the carnival.

"Yes. The Maneater killed him. . . . How did you know about the song?"

Solum tapped his forehead.

"Oh. You got it from Bunny, and the girl Kay; from their minds."

Zena sat on the bed, pressing her knuckles hard against her cheekbones. Think, think . . . oh, for guidance; for a word of advice about these alien things! The Maneater, crazed, inhuman; surely a warped crystalline product; there must be some way of stopping him. If only she could contact one of the jewels and ask it what to do . . . surely it would know. If only she had the "middle-man," the interpreter, that the Maneater had been seeking all these years . . .

*The middle-man!* "I'm blind, I'm stone blind and stupid!" she gasped. All these years her single purpose had been to keep Horty away from the crystals; he must have nothing to do with them, lest the Maneater use him against humanity. But Horty was what he was; he was the very thing the Maneater wanted; he was the one who could contact the crystals. There must be a way in which the crystals could destroy what they created!

But would the crystals tell him of such a thing?

They wouldn't have to, she decided instantly. All Horty would have to do would be to understand the strange mental mechanism of the crystals, and the method would be clear to him.

If only she could tell him! Horty learned quickly, thought slowly; for eidetic memory is the enemy of methodical thought. Ultimately he would think of this himself—but by then he might be the Maneater's crippled slave. What could she do? Write him a note? He might not even be conscious to read it! If only she were a telepath . . . Telepath!

"Solum," she said urgently, "Can you—*speak*, up here" (she touched her forehead) "as well as hear?"

He shook his head. But at the same time he picked up the check on which he had written and pointed to a word.

"Horty. You can speak to Horty?"

He shook his head, and then made outgoing motions from his brow. "Oh," she said. "You can't project it, but he can read it if he tries." He nodded eagerly.

"Good!" she said. She drew a deep breath; she knew, at last, exactly what she must do. But the cost . . . it didn't matter. It couldn't matter.

"Take me back there, Solum. You've caught me. I'm frightened, I'm angry. Get to Horty. You can think of a way. Get to him and think *hard*. Think: *Ask the crystals how to kill one of their dream-things. Find out from the crystals*. Got that, Solum?"

The wall had gone up years ago, when Horty came to the very simple conclusions that the peremptory summonses which awakened him at night in his bunk were for Zena, and not for him. *Cogito, ergo sum;* the wall, once erected, stood untended for years, until Zena suggested that he try reaching into the hypnotized Bunny's mind. The wall had come down for that; it was still down when he used his new sense to locate the trailer in which Kay was a prisoner, and when he sought the nature of Havana's dying wish. His sensitive mind was therefore open and unguarded when the Maneater arrived and hurled at him his schooled and vicious lance of hatred. Horty went down in flames of agony.

In ordinary terms, he was completely unconscious. He did not see Solum catch the fainting Kay Hallowell and tuck her under his long arm while his other hand darted out to snatch up soft-faced, tenderhearted Bunny, who fought and spit as she dangled there. He had no memory of being carried to Mon-

etre's big trailer, of the tottering advent, a few minutes later, of a shaken and murderous Armand Bluett.
He was not aware of Monetre's quick hypnotic control of hysterical Bunny, nor of her calm flat voice
revealing Zena's whereabouts, nor of Monetre's
crackling command to Solum to go to the motor court
and bring Zena back. He did not hear Monetre's
blunt order to Armand Bluett: "I don't think I need
you and the girl for anything any more. Stand back
there out of the way." He did not see Kay's sudden
dash for the door, nor the cruel blow of Armand
Bluett's fist which sent her sliding back into the corner as he snarled, "I need *you* for something, sweetheart, and you're not getting out of my sight again."

But the blacking out of the ordinary world re-
vealed another. It was not strange; it had coexisted
with the other. Horty saw it now only because the
other was taken away.

There was nothing about it to relieve the utter
lightlessness of oblivion. In it, Horty was immune to
astonishment and quite without curiosity. It was a
place of flickering impressions and sensations; of
pleasure in an integration of abstract thought, of excitement at the approach of one complexity to another, of engrossing concentration in distant and
exoteric constructions. He felt the presence of indi-
viduals, very strongly indeed; the liaison between
them was non-existent, except for the rare approach
of one to another and, somewhere far off, a fused pair
which he knew were exceptional. But for these, it
was a world of self-developing entities, each evolving
richly according to its taste. There was a sense of per-

manence, of life so long that death was not a factor, save as an aesthetic termination. Here there was no hunger, no hunting, no co-operation, and no fear; these things had nothing to do with the bases of a life like this. Basically trained to accept and to believe in that which surrounded him, Horty delved not at all, made no comparisons, and was neither intrigued nor puzzled.

Presently he sensed the tentative approach of the force which had blasted him, used now as a goad rather than as a spear. He rebuffed it easily, but moved to regain consciousness so that he might deal with the annoyance.

He opened his eyes and found them caught and held by those of Pierre Monetre, who sat at his desk facing him. Horty was sprawled back in an easy-chair, his head propped in the angle of the back and a small rounded wing. The Maneater was radiating nothing. He simply watched, and waited.

Horty closed his eyes, sighed, moved his jaws as a man does on awakening.

"Horty." The Maneater's voice was mellow, friendly. "My dear boy. I have looked forward so long to this moment. This is the beginning of great things for us two."

Horty opened his eyes again and looked about. Bluett stood glowering at him, a shuddering mixture of fear and fury. Kay Hallowell huddled in the corner opposite the entrance, on the floor. Bunny squatted next to her, holding limply to Kay's forearm, looking out into the room with vacant eyes.

"Horty," said the Maneater insistently. Horty met his gaze again. Effortlessly he blocked the hypnotic force which the Maneater was exerting. The mellow voice went on, soothingly, "You're home at last, Horty—really home. I am here to help you. You belong here. I understand you. I know the things you want. I will make you happy. I will teach you greatness, Horty. I will protect you, Horty. And you will help me." He smiled. "Won't you, Horty?"

"You can drop dead," said Horty succinctly.

The reaction was instant—a shaft of brutal hatred whetted to a razor-edge, a needle-point. Horty rebuffed it, and waited.

The Maneater's eyes narrowed and his eyebrows went up. "Stronger than I thought. Good. I'd rather have you strong. You *are* going to work with me, you know."

Horty blankly shook his head. Again, and twice more, the Maneater struck at him, timing the psychic blows irregularly. Had Horty's defense been a counter-act, like that of a rapier or a boxing-glove, the Maneater would have gotten through. But it was a wall.

The Maneater leaned back, consciously relaxing. His weapon apparently took quantities of energy. "Very well," he purred. "We'll dull you down a bit." He drummed his fingers idly.

Long moments passed. For the first time Horty realized that he was paralyzed. He could breathe fairly easily, and, with difficulty, move his head. But his arms and legs were leaden, numb. A vague ache in the nape of his neck—and his profound knowledge of anatomy—informed him of a skilfully administered spinal injection.

Kay stirred and was quiet. Bunny looked at her and away, still with that vacant gaping look on her sweet round face. Bluett shifted uncomfortably on his feet.

The door was elbowed aside. Solum came in with Zena in his arms. She was limp. Horty tried frantically and uselessly to move. The Maneater smiled engagingly and motioned with his head. "Into the corner with the rest of the trash," he said. "We might be able to use her. Think our friend would be more co-operative if we cut her down a bit?"

Solum grinned wolfishly.

"Of course," said the Maneater thoughtfully. "She isn't very big to begin with. We'd have to be careful. A little at a time." Belying his offhand tone, his eyes watched every move of Horty's face. "Solum, old fellow, our boy Horty is a little too alert. Suppose you jolt him a bit. The edge of your hand at the side of his neck, right at the base of the skull. The way I showed you. You know."

Solum stalked over to Horty. He put one hand on Horty's shoulder, and took careful aim with the other. The hand which rested on his shoulder squeezed slightly, over and over again. Solum's eyes burned down to Horty's. Horty watched the Maneater. He knew the major blow would come from there.

Solum's other hand came down. A fraction of a second after it hit his neck, Monetre's psychic bolt smashed against Horty's barrier. Horty felt a faint surprise; Solum had pulled the punch. He looked up quickly. Solum, his back turned to the Maneater, touched his forehead, worked his lips anxiously. Horty shrugged this off. He had no time for idle wonderments . . . he heard Zena whimper.

"You're in my way, Solum!" Solum moved reluctantly. "You'll have another chance at him," said the Maneater. He opened the drawer in front of him and took out two objects. "Horty, d'ye know what these are?"

Horty grunted and nodded. They were Junky's eyes. The Maneater chuckled. "If I smash these, you die. You know that, don't you?"

"Wouldn't be much help to you then, would I?"

"That's right. But I just wanted to let you know I have them handy." Ceremoniously he lighted a small alcohol blow-lamp. "I don't have to destroy them. Single-crystal creatures react beautifully to fire. You should do twice as well." His voice changed abruptly. "Oh, Horty, my boy, my dear boy—don't force me to play with you like this."

"Play away," gritted Horty.

"Hit him again, Solum." Now the voice crackled.

Solum swept down on him. Horty caught a glimpse of Armand's avid face, the flick of a tongue across his wet lips. The blow was heavier this time, though still surprisingly less powerful than he expected—less powerful, for that matter, than it looked. Horty rolled his head with the impact, and slumped down with his eyes closed. The Maneater hurled no bolts this time, apparently in an attempt to force Horty to use up counter-ammunition while saving his own.

"Too hard, you idiot!"

Kay's voice moaned out of the corner, "Oh, stop it, stop it . . ."

"Ah." The Maneater's chair scraped as he turned. "Miss Hallowell! How much would the young man do for you? Drag her out here, Bluett."

The Judge did. He said, with a leer, "Save some for me, Pierre."

"I'll do as I like!" snapped the Maneater.

"All right, all right," said the Judge, cowed. He went back to his corner.

Kay stood erect but trembling before the desk. "You'll have the police to answer to," she flared.

"The Judge will take care of the police. Sit down, my dear." When she did not move, he roared at her. "*Sit down!*" She gulped and sat in the chair at the end of the long desk. He reached out and trapped her wrist, pulled it toward him. "The Judge tells me you like having your fingers cut off."

"I don't know what you m-mean. Let me g—"

Meanwhile Solum was on his knees beside Horty, rolling his head, slapping his cheeks. Horty submitted patiently, quite conscious. Kay screamed.

"Nice noisy carnival we have here," smiled the Maneater. "That's quite useless, Miss Hallowell." He pulled a heavy pair of shears out of the drawer. She screamed again. He put them down and took up the blow-lamp, passing the flame lightly over the crystals which lay winking before him. By some fantastic stroke of luck—or perhaps some subtler thing than luck, Horty flashed a quick look through his lashes at that precise second. As the pale flame touched the jewels, he threw his head back, twisted his features—

But he did it on purpose. He felt nothing.

He looked at Zena. Her face was strained, her whole soul streaming through it, trying to tell him something . . .

He opened his mind to it. The Maneater saw his eyes open and hurled another of those frightful psychic impulses. Horty slammed his mind shut barely in time; part of the impulse got in and jolted him to the core.

For the first time he fully recognized his lack, his repeated failure to figure things clearly out for himself. He made a grim effort. Zena trying to tell him something. If he had just a second to receive her . . . but he was lost if he submitted to another such blow as the first one. There was something else, something about—*Solum!* The signalling hand on his shoulder, the hot eyes, bursting with something unsaid . . .

"Hit him again, Solum." The Maneater picked up the shears. Kay screamed again.

Again Solum bent over him; again the hand pressed his shoulder secretly, urgently. Horty looked the green man full in the eyes and opened up to the message which rolled there.

*ASK THE CRYSTALS. Ask the crystals how to kill one of their dream-things. Find out from the crystals.*

"What are you waiting for, Solum?"

Kay screamed and screamed. Horty closed his eyes and his mind. Crystals . . . not the ones on the table. The—the—*all* the crystals, which lived in—in—

Solum's hard hand landed on his neck. He let it drive him under, down and down into that lightless place full of structural, shimmering sensations. Resting in it, he drove his mind furiously about, questing. He was ignored completely, majestically. But there was no guard against him, either. What he wanted was there; he had only to understand it. He would not be helped or hindered.

He recognized now that the crystal-world was not loftier than the ordinary one. It was just—different. These self-sufficient abstracts of ego were the crystals, following their tastes, living their utterly alien existences, thinking with logic and with scales of values impossible to a human being.

He could understand some of it, untrammeled as he was with fixed ideas, though he was hammered into human mold too solidly to be able to merge himself completely with these unthinkable beings. He understood almost immediately that Monetre's theory of the crystal-dreams was true and not-true, like the convenient theory that an atom-nucleus had planetary particles rotating about it. The theory worked in simple practice. The manufacture of living things was a function with a purpose, but that purpose could never be explained in human terms. The one thing that was borne in on Horty was the almost total unimportance, to the crystals, of this function. They did it, but it served them about as much as a man is served by his appendix. And the fate of the creatures they created mattered as little to them as does the fate of a particular molecule of $CO_2$ exhaled by a man.

Nevertheless, the machinery by which the creation was done was there before Horty. Its purpose was beyond him, but he could grasp its operation. Studying it with his gulping, eidetic mind, he learned . . . things. Two things. One had to do with Junky's eyes, and the other—

It was a thing to do. It was a thing like stopping a rolling boulder by blocking it with another rolled in its path. It was a thing like lifting the brush-holder on a DC motor, like cutting the tendons at the back of the hind legs of a running horse. It was a thing done with the mind, with a tremendous effort, which said a particular *stop*! to a particular kind of life.

Understanding, he withdrew, not noticed—or ignored—by the strange egos about him. He let in the light. He emerged, and felt his first real astonishment. His neck stung from the blow of Solum's hand, which was still rebounding. The same scream which had begun when he went under came to its gasping conclusion as he came up. Bunny still stared between the slow blink of her drugged-looking lids; Zena still crouched with the same tortured expression of concentration in her pointed face.

The Maneater hurled his bolt. Horty turned it aside, and now he laughed.

Pierre Monetre rose, his face blackening with rage. Kay's wrist slipped out of his hand. Kay bounded for the door; Armand Bluett blocked her. She cowered away, across to Zena's corner, and slumped down, sobbing.

Horty knew what to do, now; he had learned a

thing. He tested it with his mind, and knew immediately that it was not a thing which could be done casually. It meant a gathering of mental powers, a shaping of the mass of them, an aiming, a triggering. He turned his mind in on itself and began to work.

"You shouldn't have laughed at me," said the Maneater hoarsely. He raked in the two jewels and dropped them into a metal ash tray. He picked up the blow-lamp, meticulously adjusting the flame.

Horty worked. And still, a part of his mind was not occupied with the task. You can kill crystal-creatures, it said. The Maneater, yes, but—this is a big thing you are going to do. It may kill others . . . what others? Moppet? The two-headed snake? Gogol? *Solum?*

Solum, ugly, mute, imprisoned Solum, who had, at the last moment, turned against the Maneater and had helped him. He had carried Zena's message, and it was his own death warrant.

He looked up at the green man, who was backing away, his flaring eyes still anxiously filled with the message, not knowing that Horty had read it and acted upon it seconds before. Poor, trapped, injured creature . . .

But it was Zena's message. Zena had always been his arbiter and guide. The fact that it was hers meant that she had considered the cost and had decided accordingly. Perhaps it was better this way. Perhaps Solum could, in some unfathomable way, enjoy a peace that life had never yielded him.

The strange force mounted within him, his polymorphic metabolism draining itself into the arsenal of his mind. He felt the drugged strength drain out of his hands, out of the calves of his legs.

"Does this tickle?" snarled the Maneater. He swept the flame over the winking jewels. Horty sat rigidly, waiting, knowing that now this mounting pressure was out of his control, and that it would release itself when it reached its critical pressure. He kept his gaze fixed on the purpling, furious face.

"I wonder," said the Maneater, "which crystal builds which part, when two of them go at it." He lowered the flame like a scalpel, stroking it back and across one of the crystals. "Does that—"

Then it came. Even Horty was unprepared for it. It burst from him, the thing he had understood from the crystals. There was no sound. There was a monstrous flare of blue light, but it was inside his head; when it had passed he was quite blind. He heard a throttled cry, the fall of a body. Slowly, then, knees, hip, head, another body. Then he gave himself up to pain, for his mind, inside, was like a field after a wind-driven brush fire, raw and burnt and smoking, speckled with hot and dying flames.

Blackness crept over it slowly, with here and there a stubborn luminous pain. His vision began to clear. He lay back, drained.

Solum had tumbled to the floor by his side. Kay Hallowell sat against the wall with her hands over her face. Zena leaned against her, her eyes closed. Bunny still sat on the floor, staring, weaving very slightly. Near the door, Armand Bluett was stretched out. Horty thought, the fool passes out like a corseted Victorian. He looked at the desk.

Pale and shaken, but erect, the Maneater stood. He said, "You seem to have made a mistake."

Horty simply stared at him dully. The Maneater said, "I would think that, with your talents, you would know the difference between a crystalline and a human being."

*I never thought to look,* he cried silently. *Will I ever learn to doubt? Zena always did my doubting for me!*

"You disappoint me. I always have the same trouble. My average is pretty high, though. I can spot 'em about eight times out of ten. I will admit, though, that *that* was a surprise to me." He tossed a casual thumb at Armand Bluett. "Oh well. Another heart case on the Fair Grounds. A dead crystalline looks just the same as a dead human. Unless you know what to look for." With one of those alarming changes of voice, he said, *"You tried to kill me . . ."* He wandered over to Horty's chair and looked down at Solum. "I'll have to learn to get along without old Solum. Nuisance. He was very useful." He kicked the long body idly, and suddenly swung around and landed a stinging slap on Horty's mouth. "You'll do twice what he did, and like it!" he shouted. "You'll jump when I so much as whisper!" He rubbed his hands.

"Oh-h-h . . ."

It was Kay. She had moved slightly. Zena's head had thumped down into her lap. She was chafing the little wrists.

"Don't waste your time," said the Maneater, casually. "She's dead."

Horty's fingertips, especially the growing stubs on his left hand, began to tingle. *She's dead. She's dead.*

At his desk, the Maneater picked up one of the crystals and tossed it, glancing at Zena. "Lovely little thing. Treacherous snake, of course, but pretty. I'd like to know where the crystal that made her got its model. As nice a job as you'll find anywhere." He rubbed his hands together. "Not a patch on what we'll have from now on, hey, Horty?" He sat down, fondling the crystal. "Relax, boy, relax. That was one hell of a blast. I'd like to learn a trick like that. Think I could? . . . Maybe I'll leave it to you, at that. Seems to be quite a drain on you."

Horty tensed muscles without moving. Strength was seeping back into his exhausted frame. Not that it would do him much good. The drug would hold him if he were twice his normal strength.

*She's dead. She's dead.* When he said that, he meant Zena. Zena had wanted to be a real live normal human being . . . well, all strange people do, but Zena especially, because she wasn't human, not at all. That was why she'd never let him read her mind. She didn't want anyone to know. She wanted so *much* to be human. But she'd known. She must have known when she sent him the message through Solum. She knew it would kill her too. She was—more of a human being than any woman born.

*I'll move now,* he thought.

"You'll sit there without food or water until you rot," the Maneater said pleasantly, "or at least until you weaken enough to let me into that stubborn head of yours so I can blast out any silly ideas you may have about being your own master. You belong to *me* —three times over." He handled the two crystals lovingly. "Stay where you are!" he snarled, whirling on Kay Hallowell, who had begun to rise. Startled and broken, she sank down again. Monetre rose, went and stood over her. "Now, what to do with you. Hm."

Horty closed his eyes, and with all his mounting energy, he thought. What was the drug Monetre had used? One of the 'ocaines, surely—benzocaine, monocaine . . . He was conscious of approaching vertigo, the first hint of nausea. Which drug would yield just this effect, then demonstrate just this much toxicity? In the back of his mind, he saw the riffling pages of a drug dictionary.

*Think!*

A dozen drugs could have this effect. But Monetre would certainly choose one that would do all he wanted—and he wanted more than immobility. He wanted psychic stimulation with it.

*Got it!* The old standby—cocaine hydrochloride. Antidote . . . epinephrine.

Now I've got to be a pharmacy, he thought grimly. Epinephrine . . .

Adrenalin! Close enough—and very easy to supply under the circumstances. He had only to open his eyes and look at the Maneater. His lips curled. The vertigo faded. His heart began to thump. He controlled it. He could feel his body going into a forced-draft condition. His feet began to tingle almost unbearably.

"You could be a heart failure case too," the Man-eater was saying pensively to Kay. "A little *curare* . . . no. The Judge is enough for one day."

Watching Monetre's back, Horty flexed his hands, pressed his elbows against his sides until his pectoral muscles crackled. He tried to rise, tried again. He all but collapsed, and then freedom and hate combined to accelerate the return of strength to his body. He rose, clenching his hands, trying not to breathe noisily.

"Well, we'll dispose of you in some way," said the Maneater, returning to his desk, talking over his shoulder at the frightened girl. "And soon—*uh!*" He found himself face to face with Horty.

The Maneater's hand crept out and closed around the jewels. "Don't come one small half-inch nearer," he rasped, "or I'll smash these. You'll slump together like a bag of rotten potatoes. Don't move, now."

"Is Zena really dead?"

"As a doornail, son. I'm sorry. I'm sorry that it was so quick, I mean. She deserved a more artistic treat-ment. *Don't move!*" He held the crystals together in one hand, like walnuts about to be cracked. "Better go back and sit down where it's comfortable." Their eyes met, held. Once, twice, the Maneater sent Horty his barbed hate. Horty did not flinch. "Wonderful de-fense," said the Maneater admiringly. "Now go and *sit* down!" His fingers tightened on the crystals.

Horty said, "I know a way to kill humans too." He came forward.

The Maneater scuttled back. Horty rounded the desk and came on. "You asked for it!" panted the

Maneater. He closed his bony hand. There was a faint, tinkling crackle.

"I call it Havana's way," said Horty thickly, "after a friend of mine."

The Maneater's back was against the wall, round-eyed, pasty-faced. He goggled at the single intact crystal in his hand—like walnuts, only one broke when the two were crushed together—uttered a bird-like squeak, dropped the crystal, and ground it under his feet. Then Horty had both hands on his head. He twisted. They fell together. Horty wrapped his legs around the Maneater's chest, got another grip on the head, and twisted again with all his strength. There was a sound like a pound of dry spaghetti being broken in two, and the Maneater slumped.

Blackness showered in descending streamers around Horty. He crawled off the inert figure, pushing his face almost into Bunny's. Bunny's face was looking down and past him, and was no longer vacant and staring. Her lips were curled back from her teeth. Her neck was arched, the cords showing starkly. Gentle Bunny . . . she was looking at the dead Maneater, and she was laughing.

Horty lay still. Tired, tired . . . it was almost too much effort to breathe. He raised his chin to make it easier for air to pass his throat. This pillow was so soft, so warm . . . Feather-touches of hair lay on his upturned face, delicately stroked his closed eyelids. Not a pillow; a round arm curved behind his head. Scented breath at his lips. She was big, now; a regular human girl, the way she always wanted to be. He kissed the lips. "Zee. Big Zee," he murmured.

"Kay. It's Kay, darling, you poor brave darling . . ."

He opened his eyes and looked up at her, his eyes a child's eyes for the moment, full of weariness and wonder. "Zee?"

"It's all right. Everything's all right now," she said soothingly. "I'm Kay Hallowell. Everything's all right."

"Kay." He sat up. There was Armand Bluett, dead. There was the Maneater, dead. There was—was—He uttered a hoarse sound and scrambled uncertainly to his feet. He ran to the wall and picked Zena up and put her gently on the table. She had plenty of room . . . Horty kissed her hair. He gathered her hands together and called her quietly, twice, as if she were hiding somewhere near and was teasing him.

"Horty—"

He did not move. With his back to her, he said thickly, "Kay—where'd Bunny go?"

"She went to sit with Havana. Horty—"

"Go stay with her a little. Go on. Go on . . ."

She hesitated, and when she left, she ran.

Horty heard a mourning sound, but he did not hear it with his ears. It was inside his head. He looked up. Solum stood there, silent. The mourning sound appeared again in Horty's head.

"I thought you were dead," Horty gasped.

*I thought you were dead,* the silent, startled response came. *The Maneater smashed your jewels.*

"They were through with me. They've been through with me for years. I'm grown . . . complete

. . . finished, and I have been since I was eleven. I just found out, when you sent me to—to speak to the crystals. I didn't know. Zena didn't know. All these years she's been . . . oh, Zee, Zee!" Horty raised his eyes after a bit and looked at the green man. "What about you?"

*I'm not a crystalline, Horty. I'm human. I happen to be a receptive telepath. You gave me a nasty jolt right where I felt it most. I don't blame you and the Maneater for thinking I was dead. I did myself for a while. But Zena—*

Together they stood over the tiny, twisted body, and their thoughts were their own.

After a time they talked.

"What'll we do with the Judge?"

*It's dark now. I'll leave him near the midway. It will be heart failure.*

"And the Maneater?"

*The swamp. I'll take care of it after midnight.*

"You're a big help, Solum. I feel sort of—lost. I would be, too, if it hadn't been for you.

*Don't thank me. I haven't the brains for a thing like that. She did it. Zena. She told me exactly what to do. She knew what was going to happen. She knew I was human, too. She knew everything. She did everything.*

"Yeah. Yeah, Solum . . . What about the girl? Kay?"

*Oh. I don't know.*

"I think she better go back where she was working. Eltonville. I wish she could forget the whole thing."

*She can.*

"She—oh, of course. I can do that. Solum, she—"

*I know. She loves you, just as if you were human. She thinks you are. She doesn't understand any of this.*

"Yes. I—wish . . . Never mind. No I don't. She's not my—my kind. Solum—Zena . . . loved me."

*Yes. Oh, yes . . . and what are you going to do?*

Me? I don't know. Cut out, I guess. Play guitar somewhere."

*What would she want you to do?*

"I—"

*The Maneater did a lot of harm. She wanted to stop him. Well, he's stopped. But I think perhaps she would like you to right some of the wrongs he's done. All over our carnival route, Horty—anthrax in Kentucky, deadly nightshade in the pasture lands up and down Wisconsin, puff adders in Arizona, polio and Rocky Mountain spotted fever in the Alleghenies; why, he even planted tsetse flies in Florida with his infernal crystals! I know where some of them are, but you could find the rest better even than he could.*

"My God . . . and they mutate, the diseases, the snakes . . ."

*Well?*

"Who would I be working for? Who's going to run the—Solum! Why are you staring at the Maneater like that? What's your idea? You—you think I—"

*Well?*

"He was three inches taller . . . long hands . . . narrow face . . . I don't really see why not, Solum. I could play it that way for a while—at least until

'Pierre Monetre' wound up the arrangements to have 'Sam Horton' run the carnival so he can retire. Solum, you have a brain."

*No. She told me to suggest it to you if you didn't think of it yourself.*

"She— Oh Zee, Zee . . . Solum, if it's all the same to you, I've got to be by myself a while."

*Yes. I'll get this carrion out of here. Bluett first. I'll just tote him to the First Aid tent. No one ever asks old Solum any questions.*

Horty stroked Zena's hair, once. His eyes strayed around the trailer and fixed on the Maneater's body. He walked abruptly over to it and turned it over on its face. "I don't like to be stared at . . ." he muttered.

He sat down at the desk on which Zena's body lay. He pulled the chair up close, crossed his forearms and rested his cheek on them. He didn't touch Zena, and his face was turned away from her. But he was *with* her, close, close. Softly, he talked to her, using their old idioms, just as if she were alive.

"Zee . . .?

"Does it hurt you, Zee? You look as if you hurt. 'Member about the kitten on the carpet, Zee? We used to tell each other. It's a soft carpet, see, and the kitten digs its claws in and str-r-etches. It goes down in front and up behind, and it yawns, *yeeowarrgh!* And then it tips one shoulder under and jus' *pours* out flat. And if you lift a paw with your finger it's as limp as a tassel and drops back *phup!* on the deep soft rug. And if you think about that until you see it, all of it, the place where the fur's tousled a bit, and the little line of pink that shows on the side because the kitten's just too relaxed to close his mouth all the way—why then, you just *can't* hurt any more.

"There, now . . .

"It hurt you to be different from—from folks, didn't it, Zee? I wonder if you know how much there is of that in everybody. The strange people, the little people—they have more than most. And you had more than any of them. Now I know, *now* I know why you wished and wished you were big. You pretended you were human, and had a human sorrow that you weren't big; and that way you hid from yourself that you weren't human at all. And that's why you tried so hard to make me the best kind of human you could think of; because you'd have to be pretty human yourself to do all that for humanity. I think you believed, really believed you were human —until today, when you had to face it.

"So you faced it, and you died.

"You're full of music and laughter and tears and passion like a real woman. You share, and you know about *with*ness.

"Zena, Zena, a jewel dreamed a truly beautiful dream when it made you!

"*Why didn't it finish the dream?*

"Why don't they finish what they start? Why these sketches and no paintings, these chords with no key signatures, these plays cut off at the second-act climax?

"*Wait!* Shh—Zee! Don't say anything . . .

"Must there be a painting for every sketch? Do you

have to compose a symphony for every theme? Wait, Zee . . . I've got a big think in my head . . .

"It comes straight from you. Remember all you taught me—the books, the music, the pictures? When I left the carnival I had Tchaikowsky and Django Rheinhart; I had *Tom Jones, a Foundling* and *1984.* And when I went away I built on these things. I found new beauties. I have Bartok and Gian-Carlo Menotti now, *Science and Sanity* and *The Garden of the Plynck.* Do you see what I mean, honey? New beauties . . . things I'd never dreamed of before.

"Zena, I don't know whether it's a large or a small part of the crystals' life, but they have an art. When they're young—as they develop—they try their skills at copying. And when they mate (if it is mating) they make a new something. Instead of copying, they take over a living thing, cell by cell, and build it to a beauty of their own invention.

"I'm going to show them a new beauty. I'm going to point a new direction for them—something they've never dreamed before."

Horty rose and went to the door. He pulled down the louvres and locked them, and shot the inside bolt. Returning to the desk, he sat down and went through the drawers. From the deep one at the left he lifted a heavy mahogany box, opened it with the Maneater's keys, and took out the trays of crystals. He glanced at them curiously under the desk light. Ignoring the labels, he piled all the crystals in a heap beside Zena's body, and put his head in his hands among them. It was quite dark except for the desk-lamp; very little light filtered into the draped oval windows of the trailer.

Horty leaned forward and kissed the smooth, cool elbow. "Now stay here," he whispered. "I'll be right back, honey."

He bowed his head and closed his eyes, and let his mind go dark. His sense of presence in the trailer slipped away, and he became detached, a wanderer in lightlessness.

Again another sense replaced his sight, and once again he found himself aware of Presences. Profoundly, this time, all "group" atmosphere was lacking, but for one—no, three quite distant pairs. But all the rest were single, isolated, sharing nothing, each pursuing esoteric, complicated lines of thought . . . not thought, but something like it. Horty felt the differences between the creatures sharply. One was concentrated grandeur, dignity and peace. Another's aura was dynamic, haughty, and another closely hid a strange, pulsating, secret idea-series that entranced him, though he knew he'd never understand it.

The strangest thing of all was this: that he, a stranger, was not strange among them. Strangers anywhere on earth, on entering a club, or auditorium, or swimming pool, are, to some extent, made conscious of their lack of membership. But Horty felt no trace of such a thing. And neither did he feel included. Or ignored. He knew they noticed him. They knew he watched them. He could feel it. No one here, however long he stayed, would try communication—he was sure of that. And no one would avoid it.

And in a flash he understood. All earthborn life

proceeds and operates from one command: Survive! A human mind cannot conceive of any other base.

The crystals had one—and a very different one.

Horty almost grasped it, but not quite. As simple as "survive!", it was a concept so remote from anything he'd ever heard or read that it escaped him. By that token, he was sure that they would find his message complex and intriguing.

So—he spoke to them. There are no words for what he said. He used no words; the thing he had to say came out in one great surge of rich description. Holding every thought that had been sleeping in his mind for twenty years, his books and music, all his fears and joys and puzzlements, and all his motives, this single flash of message coursed among the crystals.

It told of her perfect white teeth and her musical diction. It told of the time she had sent Huddie off, and the turn of her cheek, and the depth of expression which lay in her eyes. It told of her body, and cited a thousand and one human standards by which she was beautiful. It told of the eloquent rustling chords of her half-size guitar, and her generous voice, and the danger she faced in defense of the species denied her by one of the crystals. It pictured her artlessly naked; it brought back the difficult, half-concealed weeping; outbalanced her tears with a peal of arpeggio laughter; and told of her pain, and her death.

Implicit in this was humanity. With it, the base of Survival emerged, a magnificent ethic: *the highest command is in terms of the species, the next is survival of group. The lowest of three is survival of self.* All good and all evil, all morals, all progress, depend on this order of basic commands. To survive for the self at the price of the group is to jeopardize species. For a group to survive at the price of the species is manifest suicide. Here is the essence of good and of greed, and the wellspring of justice for all of mankind.

And back to the girl, the excluded. She has given her life for an alien caste, and has done it in terms of its noblest ethic. It might be that "justice" and "mercy" are relative terms; but nothing can alter the fact that her death, upon earning her right to survive, is bad art.

And that, in brief, all weighted down with clumsy, partial words, describes his single phrase of message.

Horty waited.

Nothing. No response, no greeting . . . nothing.

He came back. He felt the desk under his forearms, his forearm on his cheek. He raised his head and blinked at the desk light. He moved his legs. No stiffness. Some day he must investigate the anomaly in time-perception in that atmosphere of alien thought.

It hit him then—his failure.

He cried out, hoarsely, and put his arms out to Zena. She lay quite still, quite dead. He touched her. She was rigid. Rigor had accented the crooked smile resulting from the damage the Maneater had done to her motor centers. She looked brave, rueful, and full of regret. Horty's eyes burned. "You dig a hole, see," he growled, "and you drop this in it, and you cover it up. And then what the hell do you do with the rest of your life?"

He sensed someone at the door. He took out his handkerchief and wiped his eyes. They still burned. He turned out the desk lamp and went to the door. Solum.

Horty went out, closed the door behind him, and sat down on the mounting step.

*As bad as that?*

"I guess it is," said Horty. "I—didn't really think she was going to stay dead until just now." He waited a moment, then said harshly, "Make conversation, Solum."

*We lost about a third of our strange people. Every one of them within two hundred feet of that blast of yours.*

"May they rest in peace." He looked up at the looming green man. "I meant that, Solum. It wasn't just a line."

*I know.*

A silence. "I haven't felt like this since I was kicked out of school for eating ants."

*What did you do that for?*

"Ask my crystals. While they operate they cause a hell of a formic acid deficiency. I don't know why. I couldn't keep away from 'em." He sniffed. "I can smell 'em now." He bent, sniffed again. "Got a light?"

Solum handed him a lighter, flaming. "Thought

so," said Horty. "Stepped smack on an anthill." He took up a pinch of the hill and sifted it on his palm. "Black ants. The little brown ones are much better." Slowly, almost reluctantly, he turned his hand over and dropped the rubble. He dusted his hands.

*Come on over to the mess tent, Horty.*

"Yeah." He rose. On his face was a dawning perplexity. "No, Solum. You go ahead. I got something to do."

Solum shook his head sadly and strode off. Horty went back into the trailer, felt his way to the back wall where the Maneater had kept his laboratory racks. "Ought to have some here," he muttered, switching on the light. Muriatic, sulphuric, nitric, acetic—ah, here we go." He took down the bottle of formic acid and opened it. He found a swab, wet it in the acid and touched it to his tongue. "That goes good," he muttered. "Now, what is this? A relapse?" He lifted the swab again.

"That smells *so* good! What is it? Could I have some?"

Horty bit his tongue violently, and whirled.

She came into the light, yawning. "Of all the crazy places for me to go to sleep . . . Horty! What's the matter? You're—are you crying?" Zena asked.

"Me? Never," he said. He took her into his arms and sobbed. She cradled his head and sniffed at the acid.

After a time, when he had quieted, and when she had a swab of her own, she asked, "What is it, Horty?"

"I have a lot to tell you," he said softly. "Mostly it's about a little girl who was an undesirable alien until she saved a country. Then there was a sort of international citizen's committee that saw to it that she got her first papers, and her husband as well. It's quite a story. Real artistic . . ."

. . . in the hospital just resting up, Bobby Baby. I guess I just cracked under the strain. I don't remember a thing. They tell me I walked out of the store one evening and was found wandering four days later. Nothing had happened to me, really nothing, Bob. It's a weird thing to look back on—a hole in your life. But I'm none the worse for wear.

But here's some good news. Old Crawly-Fingers Bluett died of a heart attack at the carnival.

My job at Hartford's is waiting for me whenever I get back. And listen—remember the wild tale about the young guitarist that lent me $300 that awful night? He sent a note around to Hartford's for me. It said he had just inherited a business worth two million and I was to keep the money. I just don't know what to do. No one knows where he is or anything about him. He's left town permanently. One of the neighbors told me he had two little daughters. Anyway he had two little girls with him when he left. So the money's in the bank and Daddy's legacy in the bag.

So don't worry. Specially about me. As for those four days, they didn't leave a mark on me; well, a little bruise on one cheek, but that's nothing. They were probably good days. Sometimes when I'm waking up, I have a feeling—I can almost put my finger on it—it's sort of a half memory about loving somebody who was very, very good. But maybe I made that up. Now you're laughing at me . . .

# BOOKS BY THEODORE STURGEON

### THE DREAMING JEWELS

Eight-year-old Horty Bluett has never known love. His parents are violent and his classmates are cruel. So he runs away and joins a carnival. Performing alongside the fireaters, snakemen, and "little people," Horty is accepted. But when he loses three fingers in an accident and they grow back, it becomes clear that Horty is no ordinary boy.

Science Fiction/0-375-70373-X

### MORE THAN HUMAN

There's Lone, the simpleton who can hear other people's thoughts. There's Janie, who moves things without touching them, and there are the teleporting twins. There's Baby, who invented an antigravity engine while still in the cradle. Separately, they are freaks. Together, they compose a single organism that may represent the next step in evolution, and the final chapter in the history of the human race.

Science Fiction/0-375-70371-3

### TO MARRY MEDUSA

Gurlick was merely a sorry specimen of Homo sapiens. But now this craven, seething, barely literate drunk has ingested a spore that traveled light years before touching down on our planet. A spore that has in turn ingested Gurlick—turned him into a host for the Medusa, a hive mind so vast that it encompasses the life forms of billions of planets.

Science Fiction/0-375-70372-1

### VENUS PLUS X

Somehow, Charlie Johns has been snatched from 61 North 34th Street and delivered to the strange future world of Ledom. Here, violence is a vague and improbable notion. Technology has triumphed over hunger, overpopulation, pollution—even time and space. But there is a change that Charlie finds even more shocking: gender is a thing of the past.

Science Fiction/0-375-70374-8

### VINTAGE BOOKS
Available at your local bookstore, or call toll-free to order:
1-800-793-2665 (credit cards only).